D0745451

Slander

Linda Lê

Calomnies

Translated by Esther Allen

UNIVERSITY OF NEBRASKA PRESS

LINCOLN & LONDON

⊗ The paper in this book meets the minimum
requirements of American National Standard for
Information Sciences – Permanence of Paper for
Printed Library Materials, ANSI z39.48-1984.

Library of Congress Cataloging in Publication Data
Lê, Linda.
[Calomnies. English] Slander = Calomnies / Linda
Lê ; translated by Esther Allen. p. cm. – (European women writers series) ISBN 0-8032-2913-5
(alk. paper). – ISBN 0-8032-7963-9 (pbk. : alk.
paper) I. Allen, Esther, 1962-. II. Title. III. Series.
PQ2672.E11303519
1997 843'.914–dc20
96-33816 CIP

Contents

Slander

To the secret of no. 406

.

I

They aren't going to leave me alone after all. ¶ Ten years
locked up in this colony of half-wits, ten years spent side
by side with psychos, spastics, dodderers, lobotomy cases,
geniuses who bungled their vocation. Ten years among
the albinos, waxen faces that come alive only to insult
me, to call me Monkey-Face during their rare moments
of lucidity. ¶ Just when I thought I was safe. Here I am,
trapped by my genes again. Now a letter comes to remind
me of the family that corroded my brain, assassinated
my youth, sabotaged my life. A letter. From a pretentious
little thing (you can see it in the large, bold handwriting,
the way she turns a phrase, the way she writes French; as
if someone like me, who learned French in the nuthouse
and only so I could ask the attendants not to hit me too
hard or to give me an extra blanket, as if *I* were capable of
appreciating all the subtleties of the beautiful French language she wields like an apprentice murderer brandishing
a kitchen knife). ¶ I've done my share of cultural spade-
work too, of course. Five years in a public library, reading
everything that passed through my hands. Culture, I told
myself, culture at all costs—the idea was to get my head
back together. ¶ Still, I feel pretty good in this library.
I sort the books by genre and put them in alphabetical
order. I move through the shelves, I inspect them, check-
ing to see whether any books are out of place. Every so
often I'm asked to throw out the old system and reclas-
sify everything. For two days I play stock boy. I pretend
to be thrilled by the new system of classification, knowing perfectly well that the whole upheaval is completely
useless and in the end everything will go back to the way
it was before. In between shelving, I can stroll around, do
nothing, smoke a cigarette in the hall. I'd rather retreat

to the far end of the library, find a hiding place, and read. I never read a book all the way through. I choose every kind of book. I go from novels to journalism to historical narratives to diaries. The main thing is to have a parade of words moving under my eyes. The librarian holds me up as an example. The madman, the loathsome, swarthy foreigner, the *métèque,* who set himself to reading books. Culture saves . . . ¶ Evenings, I go back to my room, I read while I eat, I read before I go to sleep. And to think they locked me up because my nerves were a little too highly strung. I didn't know then that there was an excellent sedative: culture. ¶ I was at peace. Alone in the world and happy about it and at peace. With the books that help me live but that my body will only tolerate every other day, like a medication that saves your life but gives you diarrhea and makes hammers pound in your skull. I was alone and at peace. And that uppity little miss had to come and torment me. Remind me that I have a family, a family that held the door of the asylum open for me, that packed me away into the asylum in Corrèze. What a joke! They must have slapped their thighs, thinking about the one they pulled over on me. ¶ Fifteen years now since we saw each other. I had quite honestly forgotten she existed. Nieces always push their way back into your memory in the end, though. As little girls they show you their bare thighs and crooked teeth, leaving behind a scent of vice nipped in the bud. When they reach the age of seduction they forget you, but at the first crisis they come to you and demand that you validate their existence. They fall back on uncle the way a diva falls back on her oldest admirer.

There's only one thing *she* and I have in common: books. That's what keeps her going, it's her business, her daily bread, her stimulant. For me, books are tranquilizers. Thanks to books, I play dead. ¶ When the family sent me off in the airplane to France, to the asylum in Corrèze, *she* was ten or twelve. She arrived in this country a few years later. She's made herself a writer. A distiller of tranquilizers. A manufacturer of sedatives. She could have contented herself with being a pimp for words and left me alone. I might even have started reading her books. But she had to come and drag me out of my hiding place. What is she looking for? You might almost think she had run out of inspiration. ¶ There's no other word for it: she has come to torment me. As if I could possibly know anything, as if my memory were intact. Ten years among madmen and suddenly I am designated the guardian of truth. She places a life, her life, in my hands. If I happen to feel like telling one story instead of another, it will change the course of that life. She's crazy, I tell myself again and again. You have to be crazy to ask a madman for directions. What has gotten into her? Is it because she loves taking risks? Is it her taste for novelistic situations? She tells me, You are the only member of this family with whom I feel like establishing a link. Establishing a link! No one talks like that! She's curious about me because I'm the only madman in this tribe who's been locked up. The others were left free to go on wreaking their havoc. ¶ It's been five days since the letter arrived and for five days I've had a headache. I don't read anymore. I scribble. As soon as I've finished my shelving, I slip back to my corner at the far end of the library and write in my notebook, a big notebook with a soft gray cover. I'm not quite sure what I'm writing. Undoubtedly a report. A report I'll be able to send her so she'll realize I'm incapable of remembering anything. I'm writing a report. On *her* life. On my life. A report on betrayal. How I was betrayed by my own. How she betrayed them in turn. As if she were avenging me. They exiled me by force. She left of her own free will, clapping her hands with delight at the prospect of an immigration that — she foresaw, she

3

hoped—would deliver her from the family heritage. I had to learn French among madmen. Meanwhile, French has become her only language, her tool, her *weapon*. The weapon she uses against her family, against the Country. Thanks to that weapon, she will always be alone. She's a *métèque*, a dirty foreigner, who writes in French. For her, the French language is what madness has been for me: a way of escaping the family, of safeguarding her solitude, her mental integrity. I have nothing to say to her. She's trying to make me her accomplice. What do I remember about her? Her skinniness, her strange hair, with reddish glints. She was always following her father around—he was her guide, her playmate, her keeper. ¶ The father, the great affair of her life.

2

The man with the dog came and knocked on my door. He knocked three times, waited a moment, then went back downstairs. Through the door I heard the dog panting. A few weeks ago, the man with the dog approached me as I was sitting on a park bench reading. I answered him sharply. He's been pursuing me ever since. I walk past him in the morning; when I go out in the evening I find him in front of my building with his big black dog on a leash. I'm afraid. I think the dog is going to jump on me one day and sink his long fangs into my neck. Last week I took my laundry to the laundromat. I didn't have enough change, so I left the dirty clothes there and went out to exchange a bill for some coins. When I came back, I put the laundry in the machine and a shirt was missing. I walked by the man with the dog on my way out. I'm convinced that he stole my shirt in order to familiarize his dog with my smell and train it to attack me. I'm not sure whether it's the dog I'm afraid of or its master. They prowl around me. I have the feeling that they're trying to tell me something, but that they won't. Since I rebuffed them, they've developed a tenacious hatred of me. Little by little, the man with the dog has broken down the distance separating me from him. The first few days he lurked in my street, then he waited in front of my building, but without ever making a gesture in my direction. Now he's come to knock at my door. He knows I won't open it. ¶ The man with the dog lurks in my street in the mornings, then disappears and doesn't reappear until evening. During the hours he does sentry duty in front of the building, I stay inside or go out only accompanied by Ricin, whom I have not yet told that the man with the dog is tailing me. All the same, he's felt the weight of the gaze that the man with the dog casts on us when we walk by him, but he considers that insistent gaze to be a manifestation of the quite normal curiosity one of my countrymen feels toward me. ¶ I've discovered that the man with the dog doesn't live in my neighborhood, he works here. At the beginning of this week, I went out carrying a bag containing two pairs of shoes with broken heels. I had spotted a small, dimly lit shoe repair shop and was walking toward it. Just as I was about to cross the street, I noticed a large black shape on the sidewalk next to the door. I recognized the big dog. The door of the shop opened. I turned around and went home. ¶ Since that discovery, I can't keep myself from walking past the shop several times a day. I'm no longer afraid of the man with the dog. At night I dream he's trying to break down my door, he's stealing my shoes for his dog to eat, but I always gain the upper hand in the end: I succeed in barricading my door or in snatching the shoe from the mastiff's jaws. ¶ In order to stop being afraid of the man with the dog, I must try to learn more about the shoe repairman. I don't dare enter his shop. I know it stays open from nine in the morning until seven in the evening. The shoe repairman gives himself only a one-hour break, which he takes between noon and three, depending on his mood and the amount of work he has done. During that hour, he walks his dog in the nearby park. While he is away, his mother watches the shop. I only noticed her very recently: a wrinkled face I surprised one day behind the shelf arrayed with shoetrees and cans of shoe polish. That day my retina registered only a single image: the very hollow cheeks of an old woman who was chewing with extreme deliberation. While the shoe repairman works, the old woman sits in the corner near the window; she does nothing, she watches her son, she feeds on his image. The old woman is no more than that wrinkled face with hollow cheeks. I've never seen her leave the

6

shop. When her son goes out, she stands guard. The shoe repairman always makes sure, when he goes to walk his dog, to leave a sign on the door giving the time he'll be back. Just once I saw the shoe repairman sitting across from his mother. They were eating their midday meal.

3

Let's go back over the story from the beginning. That morning, I wake up quite early. Everything happens as it usually does, but in a corner of the room is an object I know is going to ruin my day and my peace of mind. From my bed, I glance around the room. For fifteen years now, I've lived only in the starkest surroundings: four walls, a bed, a table, a chair, a wardrobe. All made of metal, which grates on the tile floor. When you pull out a chair it makes a hellish noise. Before everything was white. Now everything is gray, the color of the end of life. Before there were nothing but chalk masks around me. Now there are nothing but dark skins. Before I was called Monkey-Face. Now they call me the Chinamad. Lunatics at least have the virtue of being sterile, alone, without family. Here the brats howl all night long. ¶ So, that morning, I get up, I sit down at my table, I drink a cup of coffee while smoking my first cigarette. In front of me, leaning against the wall, is a letter that hasn't been opened. I found it when I came home the day before, in my mailbox, box 505, in the hall in front of the superintendent's office. A letter. I was immediately suspicious. It has been years since I received a letter. I examined the envelope, the handwriting in midnight blue ink. I went up to my apartment, the letter in my hand; I had no desire to open it. I stepped into my room. I placed the letter on the table, against the wall, without opening it, and I went to bed. It's morning: the letter is still there. I look at it as you look at someone who has come to shake your shoulder and pull you out of your sleep. It's the kind of letter that you pick up with your fingertips, telling yourself that the best thing would be to rip it to shreds—finally you open it and its contents explode in your face; you regret

8

your silly curiosity but it's already far too late. I try to forget the letter and cling to the things that make up the ordinary course of my life. I listen. Outside, nothing has changed. It's like every other morning: I hear the other residents passing in front of my room, the shuffling of their slippers. They're going to the shower. Soon, when I go, I'll find the floor sopping wet. I'll have to face the soapy water stagnating in front of the shower stalls, the smells rising out of the toilets, the dirty laundry left soaking in the sinks, the doors that don't close, the broken latches. After the shower comes the race to stake a claim on the kitchen sink. There's only one sink for three families and two bachelors. Always, a gibberish in the kitchen, squabbles in the showers. People have taken the furniture that was in the recreation room back to their rooms. Kids play jump rope in the dining room, which has been emptied of its tables. The letter with its distinguished handwriting has fallen into the middle of this mess, these smells. It is suspicious: the lined envelope, the paper with its watermark, the words written with a fountain pen, and the presence, within these walls, of the forgotten niece.

I wonder if *she* has children, a husband. If she's a housewife who writes when she has time. Or else she has lovers. She leaves her writing desk to slip into their beds. And so on. Unless she lives the life of a sensual monk, an ascetic who ponders obscenities. I have dedicated ten years of my life to madness, she will dedicate as many to writing. We are, *she* and I, the runts of the litter in this family of crazies. We were the only ones to escape, to flee from the family; instead of being saved, we turned out to be incapable of leading a normal life. The others, all the other members of that family of crazies, managed to cope in their way. They are married, have children, jobs. They aren't vegetating.

*   *   *

9

Here's how she got the idea of writing to me. It happened several weeks ago in a park. That's something we have in common, she and I: a love of enclosed places reserved for life's flotsam and jetsam. She doesn't go to parks to watch children and lovers, those whose lives are in bloom, but to spy on those who are walking on the edge, who are in decline, who have let themselves go, who are no longer on speaking terms with their malevolent brother, the pitiful self who stumbled at some point, they don't know when—day after day they try to focus their memories on that fatal moment, but in vain. ¶ She sits down on a bench and pretends to read, but she isn't reading; behind her dark glasses she watches this orgy of sterile lives. She watches the old men perusing their newspapers while sitting on rusty chairs, the old men who are short of breath but still smoke, the old men who take off their shirts to warm their meager torsos in the sun; they disrobe with difficulty, as if they'd kept their clothes on all winter like another layer of skin. ¶ That day, not long before writing to me, she was sitting on a bench, a book in her hand, spying. A man walked up to her. She hadn't heard him. He was standing behind her. He spoke to her. She jumped. For the first time, she found herself in the position of the one being spied on. That was enough to infuriate her. What irritated her even more was that the stranger had addressed her in her native language. More than anything she hated it when *compatriots* approached her on the pretext of finding themselves by chance in the same foreign land. The man was still young, he was wearing black pants and his chest was bare, his shirt thrown over one shoulder. He had a large black dog with him, on a leash. She answered him sharply. He looked at her fixedly, murmured a few words she didn't catch, then went away pulling the dog by its leash. She saw him again several times, in the Metro, in that same park, in front of her place. He no longer approached her, but limited himself to prowling around her, murmuring in the language she thought she had forgotten. She avoided going to sit in the park. He re-appeared elsewhere. She thought she could get rid of him by telling herself, I have a gift for attracting crazies. She began to believe in the law that says that those who give off a smell of madness attract crazies. It's always sickness that carries you back to the family. You make a life for yourself, you purge your mind, and one day, when you drop your guard, heredity drags you away by the feet and that's it for your composed demeanor. ¶ She had resolved to leave the question of the father hanging, and now suddenly she grows afraid. She comes to ask me for some genealogical news.

4

Ricin says, Write your uncle. To get another version of the story. Your mother might have told the truth, but it's the truth of a woman in love and you know how much credibility the memories of a woman in love have.

Ricin is my conscience, my lesson-giver, the unbearable brother who always has an insult ready. The first time we met, Ricin looked down at me from above. I was young, I had a smooth face, without wrinkles or scars. I had brought a text to the one-bedroom apartment in Gennevilliers he used as an office, a text I wanted him to publish. He sized me up at first glance: I aspired to write but hadn't yet gone through the school of pain. I had no wound to claw at, no thorn to remove, no purulence to lick clean. ¶ Ricin plays the lone wolf. He stands back. He observes the time he lives in with distrust. He writes poems, aphorisms, which he doesn't publish for fear of prostituting his pain. Ricin knows he's the victim of his own delicacy. He is the Injured Party. He writes a column for a newspaper, he founded his own publishing house, but he remains the Injured Party nevertheless. ¶ Ricin earns his living while others merely rake in the dough. Ricin writes articles while others are tools of the media. Ricin is a lover of literature. Others are ignorant at best, at worst, vultures. Ricin bleeds. He refuses to attend to his wound. He has his clan, the clan of those who bleed. He rules over this clan, beyond which he sees nothing but frivolous, greedy people. ¶ Evenings, Ricin comes knocking at my door and we go for walks through Paris. ¶ Assemble all the documents relating to the case, Ricin says. Don't go running off, head down, on a quest for your father. You'll get rid of the ghost you're lugging around on your back only to burden yourself with another ghost. What good will it do you to go off in search of another father? ¶ Your mother said, I should have left your father for your other father. I should have left my husband for the Stranger, the Love of My Life. ¶ Your mother said, The only witness to this beautiful story is your uncle, the Nutcase, the Crazy. The one who lived in an asylum in Corrèze for ten years, who was released five years ago and now lives in a former residence hall converted into a welfare hotel. The man who is the keeper of this story's truth is insane. ¶ Your mother said, Ask your uncle. He will guarantee you that your true father is the Stranger, the man who passed through, my lover for a few months and the Love of My Life. Ask your uncle. He will reveal that your true father delighted in flying from conquest to victory. You'll learn that not all fathers are losers. ¶ Mada-mother, *Madamère*, said, Remember, your uncle's mind was warped. In the Country, he often came to visit us. He spent all day sitting in an armchair staring at the blank wall. When he had his fits of crazed lunacy, he would chase me with a knife in his hand. ¶ Madamother said, It was my destiny to be surrounded by pariahs. The man with the knife was the bad seed, the family's shame, the brother who haunts our nightmares, just as my husband was the man without a cent, a disastrous marriage. The man without a cent and the man with the knife, these were individuals with whom one could not allow oneself to be seen. One of them was a dreamer who let every-one walk all over him, the other a stark raving madman. One of them lacked authority, the other lacked manners. ¶ Madamother said, By chance, the family found a way to get your uncle out of the Country and send him to the asylum in Corrèze. The family arrived in France soon after he did, but no one gave a thought to what might have become of him. ¶ Back then, in the Country, the man with the knife came to stay at the house once every two or three months. He came from the madhouse and carried a little suitcase with him. Madamother picked him up outside the asylum and housed him for several days while waiting to send him back to his family. The man with the knife spent all his time sitting in an armchair. Madamother said she was worried about his violence. In fact, she was afraid of him the way one is afraid of a judge. She tried to avoid crossing the room where he stayed, spoke only in a low voice, left the house in secret, slipping out the back door. Even now, though she hasn't seen him again and he lives far away, she still speaks of him as a dangerous individual, a criminal, a man who has always had a grudge against her life; the man with the knife, says Madamother, brings only bad memories back to her. She doesn't like to think of him, it depresses her and brings only black thoughts. ¶ It wasn't the uncle's violence that worried Madamother, but his vigilance. He was the witness to all her escapades. He sat there, he kept his ears open, and he knew about all of it. Madamother hated this madman who had enough sanity left to spy on her, to be the accountant of her betrayals. Madamother hated the uncle because he was living proof that madness was a tradition to be respected in the family. Because he reincarnated the role of the ancestor, the one who ended up chained to the back of a cage, the one whose portrait tainted the family archives.

The uncle's presence brought with it the memory of the ancestor, locked by his family into a room with closed shutters. He screamed until it seemed he would die from screaming. The house was surrounded by an immense garden, so no one in the surrounding area could hear his screams. One night, the madman succeeded in prying open the shutters and escaping. He climbed up a tree in the garden and began to sing. It was the night of a lunar eclipse, utterly black. Once the family had located the madman, they had to wait for him to grow tired and decide to come down. A servant climbed the tree but didn't manage to persuade his half-naked master to come down from the branch where he was gobbling up leaves and fat red ants. After that night's adventure, the ancestor became more extravagant. His family locked him up in his room once more, but this time they barricaded the windows and boarded up the shutters. The madman no longer tried to escape. He found another source of entertainment: when they brought him his meals, he would bite the servants so hard he drew blood. A relative who owned a zoo offered the use of a cage, which was duly delivered and assembled inside the room. The ancestor was locked up inside it and, for greater security, a chain was placed around his foot, a chain long enough to allow him to come and go. That way the servants could bring him his meals without being attacked. Once a week, the ancestor was bound to the bars of the cage while a servant cleaned the excrement off the floor. To silence the rumors about the mental state of the master of the house, the family declared that the ancestor was dying, then dead. The burial was the great event of the town that month. For years the family sent flowers to the empty tomb and a gardener was sent to maintain it. As for the ancestor, he lived to a very old age, chained up at the back of his cage. When he died, he was hastily buried in the garden. ¶ Since then, it's as if each member of the family carried within himself a little cage where a demented man is chained. From time to time, the madman escapes and tramples the nerves of his descendents. Since then, everyone in the family experiences brief eclipses of consciousness. Every generation sacrifices one of its own so that the others can lead their lives sheltered from the threat of madness. Every generation designates the one who will be the acknowledged madman. The others make a show of their extreme prudence, conform to what they believe to be the rules of normal life, save face. The man with the knife has been sacrificed. He's the one who passes for crazy in the eyes of the world. The one who takes all the stigma upon himself, who clears the others of the suspicion of being deranged.

5

I don't know if I'll ever be able to lift my nose from the
dungheap of my self. My path through life has been nothing but a series of falls, collapses, missteps; each time
I had to play tricks on myself, convince myself that I
needed to pick myself back up. I played the madman
so I wouldn't go mad. I defend myself, protect myself,
like a bird that sits on her egg (even if it's rotten). The
least sound, the least movement by one of my fellow creatures is a blow to my integrity. I came to abhor madmen
whose knowledge of language was limited to ramblings,
digressions, monosyllables, infinite repetitions, insults,
and shouts. Now I've come to abhor the mentally healthy.
They sputter out words that mean nothing and they expect to receive insignificant words in return. Certain
mornings, all the noises exasperate me, make my head
ache: a door slamming, a kid crying, a negro drumming
on the kitchen table. All the noises clash and *crash* into
each other in the echo chamber of my head. Silence!
Silence! I escaped from the madhouse. It's among the
sane that my nerves will finally come unhinged. I don't
lift my nose from the dungheap of my self. But the others
make themselves forget the dungheaps they're sitting on,
they fill their ears with noises, parade images in front of
their eyes. Silence! Silence! Don't anyone say a word! Be
quiet! Anyone who feels like speaking must do no more
than whisper. Certain days, my fellow creatures' noises,
the noises that reveal life, fill me with horror. Those days,
I stay in bed, clenched into a ball, I plug my ears to block
out the sounds of life that pour out around me, this ava-
lanche of trivial signs. I huddle up, I say, Shh! Shh! I
don't want to hear the healthy-minded people who wash,
scrub, purge, and attend to the upkeep of their bodies.

17

During those moments, all languages are unbearable to me. In French or in Barbarian, all the chitter-chatter only serves to disguise the vanity of survival. ¶ Lately I don't read anymore. I've started to draw. I make pencil sketches. At the library, when I've finished with the shelving, I go off by myself with my box of supplies. I draw naked, bony bodies. The librarian watches me with concern. She doesn't like my drawings. It's unusual, she says. In fact, she's horrified. She thinks, He draws like a madman. A drawing I've just finished particularly frightens her. It shows a skinny young girl with long, drab hair. She's undressing. All her sensuality is in her open mouth, her blind eyes. Some men are in a circle around her; only their faces are visible. They avoid staring at the little girl's nakedness. Madmen know what love, sensuality are worth. They turn away. The librarian looked at the drawing and made a face of disgust. I tell her I'm going to title it "Striptease in Ward 6." "Ah! Chekhov . . ." she exclaims. But the cultural alibi isn't enough to sweep away her disturbance. ¶ I can't reveal to the librarian that the author of the letter with the distinguished handwriting is the person who inspired this drawing. I have no memories of *her* so I invent them. She often wore a sleeveless pink dress. The top of the dress fit tightly around her skinny, narrow body. The skirt was flared, with little pleats. The dress had one distinctive feature: the front was decorated with white lace panels that looked like two open curtains on her chest, and little white pearls hung from the end of the lace. When she moved or turned around the pearls made little jumps on her chest and captivated my gaze. During my stays with her family, I almost always saw her in that dress. She liked to come and rub up against me, ask me questions, sit on my lap. Her mother forbade her to speak to me—when she had to leave the house, she called her daughter and ordered her not to go near the madman, to shut herself away in another room. I

heard her whispers, her warnings, to which the little
girl made no reply. After the mother left, the house became very silent. For long minutes she didn't move from
her assigned place. Then I heard the door opening, little
footsteps coming toward me. I stayed in my armchair,
motionless. Without a word, she came to sit at my feet
and waited for me to bend down, pick her up, and set her
on my lap. She pressed herself against me and went to
sleep immediately. At other times, she told me the story
of a blind man who lived with his granddaughter in an
abandoned train car on a battlefield. ¶ There is a thread
that attaches me to her, but I broke it fifteen years ago.
I remember the day, the moment when the thread was
broken. I remember the entire episode very precisely. We
were alone, sitting in the big chair I always used when
I came to her parents' house, my hands resting on the
chair's arms. She was in my lap, facing me. She was wearing the dress with the pearls. She was telling me the next
installment of the story of the blind man and his granddaughter. Her chest was swelling, the seams of her dress
looked as if they were about to tear. My gaze was captivated by the pearls hanging from the end of the white
lace. I stretched out my hand and grasped one of the
pearls — I pulled it off. The pearl tore away from the lace
and rolled to the ground. I grabbed another which came
off in the same way and fell without a sound. I pulled off
all the others, which fell and scattered across the red and
yellow tiles like little marbles. She looked at my hand;
she didn't move. I could feel her leg muscles stiffen on
my thighs; she hadn't interrupted her narrative, she continued to tell it in a mechanical and somewhat hesitant
voice. She spoke like a person who has difficulty breathing. Her mother saved us. Hearing her mother's voice,
she jumped down, quickly gathered up the pearls, and
ran out of the room. When I got up, I saw that a pearl was
lodged in the armchair. I picked it up and kept it. Not

long after that episode, which remained a secret between her and me, the family sent me off in an airplane. I left the Country to be locked up in that asylum in Corrèze.

I try to form an image of her as she is now, fifteen years later. I remember what her mother was like at twenty-five: a stupid, capricious sphinx whose mystery lay in her ability to stop every passing man in his tracks simply by lifting her eyes to him. She was a killer doll with soft skin, long legs, firm breasts, lips painted a purplish red. She had lovely feet — they were soft and delicate, because *she never touched the ground, she walked only on the heads of human beings.* When her husband was around, she played the role of an irritatingly conformist bourgeois housewife, but in a hotel room with her lovers she was a courtesan who had a very hearty appetite for bed. Her one ambition was to be a kept woman. Since she had married a man with a meager salary, she made it up to herself with her lovers. She was one of those women whose sensuality is greatly heightened by the sight of a piece of jewelry for which a large amount of money has been paid. At twenty-five, the mother was a mulish, scandalmongering female, enormously vain and crassly ignorant, at once snobbish and illiterate; she spoke several languages but could neither read nor write any of them. The little education she had received she reserved for the life she lived outside of her house. Then she made herself up, perfumed herself, she played the elegant lady, the young woman of good family who knew how to behave at table, who spoke in a sweet voice, batted her eyelashes, knew when to say nothing and, from time to time, heaved a sigh that made her breasts quiver beneath her silk bodice. As soon as she was back in her own house, she removed her make-up, undressed, stripped off her good manners, lost the sweet voice, donned an old yellow satin outfit that smelled of sweat and had a filthy collar, plopped onto her bed, a plate of sweets within reach, and reserved the spectacle of her vulgarity for her husband. At twenty-five, the mother was sugary, plump, and voluptuous. At twenty-five, the mother was honey and gall, drug and poison. At twenty-five, the mother was a woman.

6

The Counselor says, I'm making you an honest proposal. A bell rings. The Counselor interrupts himself. A call on the author line; he picks up the second receiver, a minute goes by, then again the Counselor's voice at the other end of the line. Just one episode, he says. The show will be called *The Love of Their Life*. It will be good practice for you, the Counselor says again. You've indulged in sadness long enough. Put your corpses away. Write some exercises in jubilation. Stop slandering yourself, slandering *us*. Then the Counselor says I should write something about my father, take the money and go back to the Country. I say, Yes. The Counselor lets on that it's a nice little windfall. I say, Yes. The Counselor suggests that I draw up a proposal, two pages, and invites me to come and see him in the office he has set up, the office of his production company. I say, Yes. Use it to go back to the Country, the Counselor says three times. I say, Yes. I think of the title of a film, *We Can't Go Home Again*. In my head, the Counselor's phrase is slightly modified and I hear, *You Can't Go Home Again*. The Counselor has hung up the phone. ¶ That afternoon I sit down at my table and write two pages. When Ricin knocks at my door, I slip the text into the pocket of my coat before following him out. We walk toward the Invalides, muffled up in our coats. The beginning of a song runs through my head:

I'm a stranger here,
I'm a stranger everywhere,
I would go home, but
I'm a stranger there.

I give Ricin the text written that afternoon. Maybe I should give it to the Counselor in order to take advantage

of the windfall and go back to the Country. Ricin refuses
to read the two pages. You're using your father for your
own publicity, like a nun who always keeps a photo of an
orphan under her robe to bring out whenever her sin-
cerity is questioned. You deserve to be sentenced to spend
fifty days with your hands tied, as Japanese painters used
to have to do, in order to learn not to dissipate yourself.
You're looking for a father, you're looking for a love,
you're looking for any good reason to turn away from your
task. You write like a pitiful little man who's decided to
go on a bender. The morning after, he sticks two fingers
down his throat, vomits up the best part of himself and
goes back to his ordinary life. What you want to do demands only one thing from you: vulgar tenacity. You have
to grab the world by the balls and never let go. ¶ Again,
Ricin says, Don't expect anything from other people.
Their aim is to make you disgorge your entrails, yield up
your snot, your shit. And when there's nothing left of you
but a skeleton, a carcass that's been thoroughly picked
over, they'll take you under their protective wing. They'll
force their food down your throat, turn you into a goose
fattened on their idiocy and then think, gazing at you
with fatherly eyes, that you've given the best of yourself.
Everywhere you go, be like a dog in a china shop. Keep to
yourself. Keep on being a *métèque,* a swarthy barbarian.
Cultivate the margins, work the edges. Make sure you
always have something undesirable inside you, something
uncongenial, irreducible.

I ask for nothing more than to play the mangy dog. *Two
souls, alas, share my breast between them.* I live under the
piercing, watchful eye of an elder brother who will tolerate no cowardice, no compromise, who does what he
can and derives no satisfaction from it. The problem is
that there isn't only this ascetic elder brother, there's also
me. The puppet greedy for success, the piece of fluff that

would like to be a gaudy bird preening its feathers for a large audience. For the moment, the elder brother is holding me back. But I have to be careful; the vain doll wants to escape, talk loudly, and do her number far away from this old, wet blanket of a brother.

7

Everything tells her to turn away from the father, convinces her that she'll only find her salvation by freeing herself from all ties to her progenitors. But she wants to go on letting herself be consumed by the ghost of the father. Before, she was haunted by the father she thought she had betrayed and abandoned. Now, she has provided herself with a new father, and suddenly she's the abandoned one. There's no doubt this new role suits her better: she has always enjoyed playing the wounded diva, the visionary victim, the Saint Sebastian of the familial disorder. Her mother's revelation had no other goal but this: to consume her with doubts, to riddle her with uncertainties. Her mother succeeded where all the philosophy books failed. In a single sentence her mother pulverized her father's body, killed the *idée fixe*. Her mother wants only one thing: to drive her mad by making her wonder endlessly about her birth, about the identity of her true father. For years the mother has tried unsuccessfully to gain influence over her. She always slipped out of her reach, she always knew how to escape. This time the mother has her. That's why she's come to me. She hopes I'll give her the antidote to the poison that is her mother. ¶ She prowls around me. The smell of my blood attracts her — my blood that has gone sour, that has spoiled, my infected blood, my blood sick from solitude, my blood that acts proud and holds back its sobs. ¶ Who is weeping in my blood? Who? she wants to know. I'll have to tell her all the dirty laundry from the asylum. My memories give off a stench. I've always lived among odors, among a rather unappetizing portion of humanity. A humanity that smells of piss and has stinking armpits, shits in its pants and doesn't wash its crotch. Therein lies the difference between her and me: she knows only the humanity of young ladies. The young lady wants to escape from her clean walls and come sniffing around my trough. Over here, the bad smell, the gruel, the mashed-up guts, the hearts that were ripped out, the lives chopped up on the butcher's block. ¶ I'll have to tell her all the dirty laundry, the years spent sorting out dirty laundry in the asylum. In exchange for the closet I was given in the attendants' wing, I had to perform a task, give evidence of my aptitude for sanity. I reigned over the antechamber of the washhouse. Cartloads of dirty laundry would arrive. My work consisted of pawing through the nauseating pile, pulling out each piece and separating the laundry into three large baskets. In the first, I threw the dirty laundry, stained with blood, snot, spittle, excrement, semen. The second basket was for laundry that was only a little dirty, which gave off a heady smell of urine, sweat, and badly washed skin. A few pieces of laundry that were almost clean remained, and these were destined for the third basket and were often used again without having been washed. (In the same way, I separated the madmen into three categories: those who had been badly soiled by their disease, those who merely smelled of madness and those who, barely speckled with it, could still be made use of. I sorted the laundry exactly as I had been sorted out myself before being authorized to return to the margins of the rational world — declared able to be made use of again, I was part of the third basket.) My days were spent between the sour smell of laundry and the burning steam that came out of the washhouse. In winter, I would open the door to get a little of its heat. In summer, I worked stripped to the waist, the smell of dirty laundry permeating my skin, lodging in my nostrils. Everything I touched, ate, or drank stank of the snot and excrement of madmen. The hot steam made me sleepy, my eyes would often close and my head fall against the big basket. From the pile of dirty laundry, voices rose. I heard the panting of a woman being strapped down who fought until she choked on her own anguish. The smell of madmen formed images in my mind. In the hot steam coming from the washhouse, I saw mouths seeking out other mouths and not finding them, and pressing instead against the coarse pillowcases that smelled of bleach, I saw sex organs rubbing against the harsh sheets. I saw rows of beds and bodies suffocated by solitude. I saw the prickly electricity that thrilled their skins and ran, sterile, from one cot to the next.

8

Ricin is constantly telling me, Sabotage the Counselor's plans. Don't let him talk you into writing an episode of *The Love of Their Life*. You must not make yourself into the hack screenwriter of a family secret. The Counselor wants to pass you off as his protégée—the writer who is a native of the former colonies, the little starving bird, the fragile young woman he has taken up. Don't forget that foster parenthood is the great fantasy of the newly rich. In every country in the world, you'll find parvenus who write their name, address, and bank account number on a piece of paper that they tear off along the dotted line; they set themselves up as tutor, foster parent, and in exchange for a completely negligible monthly sum, the equivalent of what they spend feeding their dog, they feel entitled to receive from a Third World orphan or widow, citizen of a tropical city with an unpronounceable name, a long letter every month and a lifetime of gratitude. The ranks of foster parents dug up by humanitarian organizations include only parvenus who, rather than buying themselves a nice bottle of something or other, treat themselves to the luxury of giving a twist to the fate of a little negro boy escaped from a brothel or a garbage picker taken in by missionaries. We'll never know what it is that pushes those foster parents to act. Is it because the misery of their fellow creatures haunts their nightmares? Is it to chase from their heads the image of those millions of wretches unleashed on nature who threaten to invade the land of their foster parents if they don't receive subsidies in their own lands? Or is it only because foster parentage is the sign that they have arrived at the rung on the ladder where one becomes concerned with one's inner life and spiritual development, where one must make a show of extending one's hand beneath one? There would be a lot fewer of these false foster parents if they weren't incited to their charitable debaucheries by the shanty-town celebrities. Those clowns deserve to be shot. They proclaim themselves the special envoys of planetary suffering, don their firebrand costumes and go off to bathe in exotic misery. Once there, they ask some people to tell the story of their route to Good Samaritanhood, others to describe a day at the garbage dump in all its details. They return from their visit with an enormous brick of a book which, they say, tossing their white manes for the cameras, is a document of the courage of some—the anonymous Samaritans—and the misery of others, the millions of wretches. The shanty-town celebrities quickly add that they will donate a portion of their royalties to those humanitarian organizations that court them most skillfully and offer them a place among their founding members. So, for years, decades, the shanty-town celebrities don't have to do anything but manage the profits generated by the journey they never fail to describe as *hallucinatory*. At every earthquake, every flood, every *coup d'état* in the country of the millions of wretches, the shanty-town celebrities reappear; it's their responsibility to count the dead and remind us that despite these scourges the population is far from decimated. ¶ Ricin vomits out his rage because he is afraid of getting to the heart of the matter, the tight knot that fills his stomach with poison and gives his words their sting. I say to Ricin, You've got to lick your wound, renounce your obsession. You're living out a sham. You play the dispenser of justice, you condemn, you accuse, you claim to be humiliated, outraged, because once someone spat in your grandmother's face. (Ricin murmurs between his teeth, No one would ever have spat in her face if the Parisian journalist hadn't come to tempt her with visions of glory and then left her to deal with the scandal alone.) Your grandmother knew what she was risking.

She should have responded to those who spat in her face with her own contempt. She died because rather than spitting back at them or buying a gun and firing into the crowd, she hunched her shoulders, she walked with her back stooped beneath the jeers, she let herself be buried under the insults. ¶ For Ricin, the thing is simple: his grandmother was the victim of the Parisian journalist's wiles. His grandmother believed the Parisian journalist's speeches about the truth which must be brought out into the light of day. Ever since then, Ricin has nourished a tenacious hatred for Parisian journalists, to the point that he himself has become a Parisian journalist, half out of self-disgust and a desire to punish himself, and half from weakness and because he knows he is incapable of doing anything else. ¶ The Parisian journalist laid siege to his grandmother's house for days, weeks; she convinced his grandmother of the usefulness of true life testimonials, she persuaded her of the importance of her disclosures. She deceived her, she trapped her. I say to Ricin, You're telling yourself stories. You know perfectly well that your grandmother agreed to do it when the Parisian journalist hinted that she would make a lot of money by doing it. You know perfectly well that your grandmother acted out of vanity and greed. You want to believe she was a victim. I think she died of spite, not of shame; it was her fury at having been tricked by the Parisian journalist that killed her. And you've guessed all that: that's why you were the one who forced her to leave the house, confront the gaze of the others, allow them to spit in her face. You foresaw all of it; you wanted to punish her for her vanity. Your will to mete out justice dates from that moment. ¶ The Parisian journalist turned out to be quite an operator. Your grandmother thought she saw an opportunity to acquire some ephemeral fame, and she knew that fame doesn't come without scandal. She believed that this fame would get her out of her rut, make her the victim all Paris was talking about, but she miscalculated. The Parisian journalist deceived her victim, pocketed the money, made a reputation for herself as an unearther of petty scandals, and sent your grandmother flowers to thank the actress who played her role too well. Your grandmother wasn't a victim. She lost the war. ¶ Ricin tells me I'm taking an ax to his mental organization, I'm demolishing him, but in a sweet voice, with my hand gently resting on his shoulder. *You're nothing but a killer decked out in sweetness and light.* He walks away from me with quick steps and disappears, leaving me there by myself at one in the morning in the rue des Juges Consuls. ¶ Ricin fled to save his story. The story of an old widow who lived in a provincial city. Her grandson visited her from time to time; they took walks together. A Parisian journalist came to spend her vacation in the city and met the old widow who took advantage of the opportunity to bemoan her fate: she had always lived in this city, had always endured life in this hole, had always hated the successive generations of its inhabitants. The journalist went back to Paris. She returned several months later and suggested to the old woman that she confide the secret details of her life to the readers of the journalist's newspaper; she asked her to say all the bad things she thought about her city, the city she had never left. The old woman believed that her fate would be altered, that fame would grant her a change of scene. For two weeks, she told the Parisian journalist everything. She spoke of her youth, her desire to be an actress, the city in which she was suffocating. She told how her father had abused her when she was thirteen years old, how he had then forced her to get married and live nearby with her husband and children. The journalist returned to Paris and wrote an article inspired by the widow's confidences and fleshed out with reflections on the condition of women at the end of the last century and the narrow-mindedness of the provinces. The journal-

31

ist became briefly famous, was the object of everyone's attention, and the old widow did, too, but the attention she received came only from the residents of her city. She wrote to her grandson that she no longer left her house out of fear of reprisals. Ricin was fifteen years old at the time. He went to his grandmother's house immediately and found her in bed with the shutters closed. He opened the windows, forced his grandmother to get dressed, fix her hair, and go out to confront the city. Every day, at five in the afternoon, the old widow, on her grandson's arm, walked across the city under a hail of insults and gibes from its inhabitants. Years after his grandmother's death, Ricin still sees her in dreams, walking, her head enveloped in a scarf, on the arm of a teenager. Ricin calls these penitential walks the ceremony of jeers. After two weeks, the grandson had to leave and the old widow shut herself in her house again. Six months later, she called her grandson on the telephone, told him she was going to die, and hung up. ¶ Since then, Ricin is certain of one thing: it is Paris, it is journalists, it is young, pretty women avid for success that killed his grandmother. Not only killed her but exposed her to universal contempt. He thinks, They made her say she was her father's whore, her husband's slave; under pretext of serving truth, they dragged her through the mud, they convinced her to roll in the mud. After having been the victim of her father, her husband, provincial narrow-mindedness, my grandmother, says Ricin, was the victim of frivolous people, people who are always trying to find themselves a victim to protect, to exhibit at the county fair of injustices, a victim whose catalogue of mistreatments they itemize for an audience of torturers who missed their calling. Wounded, hunted victims, who have survived in spite of everything, are always in style. All we want is to verify that the human being is an animal with tough skin. We want to see a man who survives everything. We need a victim who struggles, who survives, who overcomes his humiliation. No one is interested in a victim who remains a victim. Styles change, and variety matters in the choice of victims, too. There are victims who died not from the mishandling of their torturers but from having been noticed, exhibited at the county fair of injustices only to be tossed aside when the diversion ceased to be amusing and the crowd began to clamor for the next act. You should understand that more than anyone. Remember when your people began to leave the Country. The fugitives piled by the hundreds into little boats as fragile as giant matchboxes. They crossed the ocean on those boats. Back here, people rubbed their hands together. They had found the ideal victims, and they called them freedom fighters. Why, the frivolous people were just about ready to run to their yachts and go rescue the victims. They piled into boats in their turn, overloaded with cameras and photographic equipment, fighting to get the first shots of those victims *with such sweet, sad eyes.* Then styles changed. Other frivolous people had tracked down new victims. So there they were, stuck there with all the extras of a megaproduction filmed on the high seas. Whatever money could be made from the adventure had already been made, and no further expenses could be run up. But what to do about the extras? They found themselves adorning the sets of another megaproduction, this one filmed not on the high seas but in camps facing the sea and surrounded by barbed wire. No one was moved by the concentration-camp decor, or by the fact that the megaproduction was entitled *The Undesirables* and its theme was the forced repatriation of the extras who had been left stranded when the stars of the megaproduction packed their bags and moved on. From time to time, footage of the film-in-progress arrived, and the extras, previously known as the freedom fighters, could be seen parading under the banner of *Freedom or Death*; the list of extras that had to be forcibly repatri-

33

ated was also shown and it was known that certain extras committed suicide when they learned they were to be included in the next convoy. Styles had changed—the frivolous people couldn't do anything about it. Their feelings, they said, followed the latest news. Every day they stuffed their faces with as much of the latest news as they could take; they couldn't go back in time just to get slapped by anachronistic emotions.

9

She pretends to be seeking the truth when she's only demanding her share of the lie. She wants me to tell her
stories, to irrigate her head with a new source of obsessions, to substitute an illusion forged by my imagination
for an illusion she created for herself and has carefully
tended for years. She believed she loved her father, but
she was only telling herself about a love she felt for an
illusion called Father. Over time she grew tired of this
and began to feel the need for a new source of excitement.
And so her mother, as if by deliberate coincidence, pro-
vides her with another father to dress up. This one has the
advantage of being a stranger—lost from sight, vanished
into thin air. His portrait can be summed up in a few
known characteristics. A father about whom she knows
nothing and whom she uses as a new cog to repair her
mirage generator, which for some time now has been spinning uselessly. The reign of Illusion I has come to an end;
that of Illusion II is beginning. What is she imagining?
That she'll be able to exhibit herself with two fathers, one
of them nailed to the soil of her native country, the other
a foreigner in transit. The martyr and the high-stakes
gambler. The failure and the seducer. On the one hand,
the husband, clinging to his homeland and his bad luck,
on the other, the visitor who never really enters the picture, only leaves with his head held high. Her mother has
dumped the two portraits down in front of her. All she
has to do is choose. Between the nonentity living under
a dark cloud that no miracle has succeeded in scrubbing
away and the savior who parachuted down in the middle
of a war to tag her—the prodigal child—with an international first name . . . ¶ Her mother says, Your real father
had perfect manners. (They would meet regularly in a

luxury hotel. A room that had been requisitioned for the officer's pleasure.) ¶ Her mother says, A true gentleman. (She would sit on the edge of the bed; he would stand facing her, bend one knee to the floor, lean down. She would raise the hem of her dress slightly. Gently, he would take hold of her ankle, remove the shoe, kiss the foot.) ¶ Her mother says, A first-class lover. (With his left hand he caressed the leg of his great wartime love, but his right hand never forgot that there was also a victory to be won—he would snap his fingers and hundreds of bombs would rain down on the Country.) ¶ Her mother says, A sensitive, delicate man. (During the days he was on leave, he shut himself with her in the hotel room, let the ceiling fans turn, listened to music until late at night, read poetry while drinking champagne. Once the rest period was over, he closed the book, put the records away, left the hotel room, and gave the order for the Country to be cleaned up, for executions to take place at regular intervals. To block out the sound of the bullet fired into the head of a guerrilla, this sensitive man would recite to himself a poem by Emily Dickinson, *A coffin—is a small Domain.*) ¶ Her mother says, A man of taste. (He gave her jewelry and silk dresses, records and rare delicacies. As she dizzied and intoxicated herself on frivolities, he would read George Bernard Shaw, *The Intelligent Woman's Guide* . . .) ¶ Her mother says, A man of taste. (After his final departure from the Country, he sent soldiers bearing thick envelopes to the home of his wartime love. The husband, the nonentity, watched his wife smile as she received those envelopes, which contained wads of bills. The man of taste was paying for the pleasures he had enjoyed. He was buying her silence; she believed he was showing his affection.) ¶ Her mother says, A man full of pride and courage. (The man of courage braved ambushes, defied snipers, visited the front lines, but he beat a hasty retreat as soon as he was threatened with fatherhood. He said, I

36

cannot know if this child is mine or your husband's — my
enemy's. The man of courage dropped out of the game.
Before leaving the Country, he chose an international first
name for the unborn child. Later, he grew brave enough
to send her a pink layette.)

IO

It's Sunday. Yesterday I bought two tickets for D. I intend to drag Ricin there with me. I won't tell him where we're going. He'll find out on the platform or maybe only once we're in the train. He'll stand up, act like he wants to get off the train; the whole trip he'll look out the window and mutter between his teeth, For nothing in the world will I set foot in that city where even the dogs are pretentious and the sand is futile. ¶ It's late autumn. The Gare Saint-Lazare is deserted. I'm waiting for Ricin in front of a newsstand. I see a large black dog emerge from a corridor; he crosses the station hall and heads for the platforms. I hear someone whistling not far from me. I look around for the dog's owner, I have the feeling he's hiding in the corridor. I listen carefully. The unknown man whistles a short, staccato tune. I watch the spot where he will appear. A man walks out of the corridor toward me. Ricin is wearing jeans, a bulky ribbed sweater under a pea coat. I ask him, Did you see anyone in the corridor? He didn't notice anything. I point out the black dog moving back and forth across the station hall. Look, it looks like the shoe repairman's dog. I don't hear the whistling anymore. I pull Ricin after me. He follows me without lifting his eyes to the sign that indicates the train's destination. ¶ This smells like enemy territory, Ricin hisses at me on our arrival in D. We take the road to the beach. Ricin accuses me of having belleletristic caprices; vehemently he tells me that he is revolted beyond anything by the adolescent mania for going to see the sea, taking the train or the car, as if there were an urgent need to escape from the city and plunk yourself down on a gray, sad beach, to walk along shivering with bloodless lips and eyes full of sand. He says, You're too old for seaside jaunts and

not old enough to make pilgrimages to the sites of your
love affairs. ¶ Near the boardwalk I think I see a black
shape darting among the cabanas. I sit down beside Ricin
with my back to the city. It's the third time I've been
to D. At my side, Ricin is the successor to Bellemort and
Weidman.

Bellemort had never been to D. in the wintertime. He
took me there one January Saturday on the evening train.
The idea was to have Sunday afternoon tea in the bar of
the city's grand hotel. Bellemort had reserved a room. We
stayed there for ten minutes, after which Bellemort called
the hotel desk to tell the young man in the black suit that
the yellow-flowered wallpaper was giving him a migraine.
The young man in the black suit showed us another room
which appeared to satisfy Bellemort. A quarter of an hour
later, the bellboy brought us our scanty baggage, but we
had already decamped — Bellemort had noticed that the
doors of the old armoire squeaked and the squeaking got
on his nerves. The young man in the black suit led us
to the top floor, to a room whose walls were lined with a
cream-colored fabric, directly under the mansard roof.
Bellemort noted the absence of an armoire with relief;
there was only a closet near the doorway. The young man
in black thanked us, assured us that he was completely at
our disposition, then went off in search of the bellboy who
was wandering from floor to floor with our baggage. The
young man had barely shut the door behind him when
Bellemort was already summoning him back: he had hit
his head against the mansard roof. We couldn't stay in
that room; the angle of the ceiling made him walk with
his back bent, in constant fear for his head. The young
man in black led us down several floors, to a room in
every respect similar to the first one, except that the wallpaper flowers weren't yellow but an almost mauve pink.
There was a sudden gleam of joy in Bellemort's eye. He

found the room to his liking. The bellboy was able to put the luggage down at last. It was midnight. The next day, Bellemort confessed to me that he had come to D. several years before to wind up a relationship that had, over time, revealed itself to be deficient in unexpected new twists. He had spent the night of the final goodbyes in the room with the mauvish pink–flowered wallpaper. Lying there beside the young woman, he was torn between the desire to strangle her and the fear of falling asleep and carrying out his desire to commit murder.

The second time, I went back to D. with Weidman. I stayed there for three days. Of the first day we spent together, I remember only having seen in an artist's studio some paintings of elongated women dressed in black; they had disproportionate bodies—gigantic, monstrous heads, and reedy legs, the legs of little girls stricken with polio. On the third day we had left D. and stopped at a little station whose name I don't remember; we had walked for hours on that beach, with the silhouette of an ocean liner anchored in the port of the neighboring city in the background. We fell asleep lying on the sand. The boat's whistle woke me up. I saw a man walking toward us, his back turned to the sea. I wanted to show Weidman the man who was coming in our direction, but there was no one on the beach. I remembered a photo of my father taken in the Country. In the photo, he is wearing a pair of khaki pants and a white T-shirt; he is walking barefoot, his back turned to the sea, his eyes fixed on the sand. He is wearing dark glasses. The only part of his face that can be seen clearly is his bulging forehead—there is a bump on the right side as if he had just fallen down.

Ricin says, The air here is tainted. He would like to go home, but he dawdles to *witness* the sunset. Once during his childhood he saw a film with his grandmother—

he has never been able to find its title or the director's
name. He remembers a scene in which a group of bums
treat themselves to the only show they can afford: they
sit down next to each other and watch the sun setting on
the big screen of the sky. Sometimes during the summer
Ricin and his grandmother would take their bicycles,
go out into the fields and watch the sunset. Ricin hopes
that, like his grandmother, he will have a presentiment
of his death. He would like to be forewarned an hour or
two before the fatal moment so he can go and die in a
movie theater. He would like to die alone, in a darkened
theater, facing the screen in the middle of an empty row.
He would like to die while watching the scene in *Moon-
fleet* when Jeremy Fox, in a sudden rush of sentimentality,
decides not to betray John Mohune, the little boy who is
always hanging around him, who says he is his friend and
who is undoubtedly his son. Ricin would like to die during the moment when Jeremy Fox hides the wound in his
chest, the blood all over his shirt, says goodbye to John
Mohune, promising him he will be back very soon, and
goes off in a boat.

II

There is only one true thing about her: the love she has
for her father—not the usurper with his officer's uniform and the airs and graces of a young man from a good
family, but the other one, the man who never amounted to
anything, who stayed behind in the Country, from whom
they separated her. Throughout her childhood, she heard
them laughing at him, she saw her father helplessly facing
their mockery, their put-downs. Throughout her childhood she saw him alone, without a friend, without a relative, without a family that could protect him. Throughout
her childhood, she defended her father against *them*, she
was on her father's side, against her mother's clan. And
now, now that *they* have succeeded in separating her from
her father, her mother tells her, You defended a man who
wasn't even your father. He knew you weren't his daughter. He pretended to love you because you clung to him.
He pretended. Deep inside, he saw you as nothing more
than a bastard child. Why do you think he waited ten days
before going to report your birth? During those ten days
he could have smothered you under a pillow, you were
nothing, not even listed in the archives, not even labeled.
But he didn't have the courage. So he went to report the
birth of the bastard daughter. When the clerk at the reg-
istry office asked him, Child's first name? he spelled the
international name that your true father chose. When the
clerk asked, Father's name? he gave his own name, he furnished his own address, he stated his own profession. He
put his stamp on you.

That love, *they* destroyed it. First by constantly denigrat-
ing the father, that son of a peasant, that ignoramus who
knew not a word of French, that dreamer who did nothing

but draw and paint, that incompetent who didn't understand the value of money and brought home a meager salary, who never played the petty tyrant or the authoritarian first officer. Then they decreed it necessary to separate father from daughter. The old man had to stay behind in the Country—his life was over. The daughter had her whole future ahead of her; she needed a land where she could blossom. The father had to play the proud man, to pretend that he loved his native land and that never, not even once, would he ever step outside its borders. Her mother dealt the final blow. Thanks to her mother, she received the revelation of her illegitimacy. Thanks to her mother, she could supply herself with another father. ¶ This was how, step by step, they destroyed that love, how they annihilated that man to the point of taking away his right to paternity and substituting him with a caricature of a father—a man of class, a man with perfect manners, a wonder. For years, she set her mind against *them,* she opposed all of their little schemes. Suddenly, she wavers. Without wanting to, she is becoming their accomplice.

She succeeded in cutting off all ties. The problem is that she's sentimental, full of illusions, and therefore ready to renew relations if someone suggests another image of the family to her. She very quickly understood the need to break away from her relatives, but she hopes they will prove her wrong, that one day or another they will metamorphose and present themselves to her with healthy minds—adoring books, despising money, and swearing only by art. That day, she will welcome them with tears of joy. This is the kind of illusion they can use to ensnare her and bring her back into the fold. By making her believe that they are capable of aesthetic emotions, that they are the champions of love at first sight. This is what her mother is trying to do, by offering her the model father

43

of her dreams: a father who loves music, reads a great deal of poetry, commits mass murder only when forced to, and is a doctor in civilian life. Her mother is offering her something sensational. Immediately she is ready to give up the old, worn-out model who no longer makes the sparks fly, who no longer has any magical power. Out of sentimentality, she succeeded in detaching herself from her family. Out of sentimentality, she is returning to them. Out of sentimentality, she headed in the direction of freedom. Out of sentimentality, she is retracing her steps, preparing to join the camp of those in power, the clan of the mass murderers. ¶ Still, she can't pretend to believe that this father, this brand new father her mother has procured for her, was a tourist. She can't try to represent him to herself as her mother described him: a man who came with his arms filled with gifts, his eyes burning with love and his lips greedy for kisses. She can't forget that words of murder issued from this man's mouth, that his lips which were blood red when he pressed them to his beloved's were pale and bloodless with determination when he was bellowing orders. Still and all she cannot imagine that the man's eyes saw nothing, that they were burning with love and not with the fires he started by dropping bombs. From his helicopter high above he saw shadows scattering in every direction. Once he was certain that the job was finished, he gave his pilot the order to take him back to the beloved who welcomed him in a perfumed chamber filled with music. ¶ She cannot have forgotten the ardor the family has always shown for the powers that be, for the small personages seated on their small thrones who suffer from a stiffness of the neck that forces them to look only at the small personages seated on small thrones above them without being able to direct their gaze below—what is below is not worth looking at. She cannot have forgotten that the family motto was, The powers that be are always right. That's why family

44

members have always learned foreign languages: not to broaden the horizons of their narrow minds, not to enlarge their field of vision, but to serve the powers that be—because the powers that be were foreigners. They learned foreign languages only in order to derive greater advantages from the powers that be, to ensure their privileges. They loved only, saw only the powers that be, or, at the very worst, our set. Our set, that is, the opportunistic vermin like us, half serpent, half eel, seeking their way guided by the smells of money and blood. She can't have forgotten that her family believed those who were being massacred were conspirators, skinny, ugly little men in black, come from who knows where. She can't have forgotten that her mother used to say that the villagers who had their bellies ripped open, the peasant women who got themselves raped, should just stop living in the country. In the cities there was no danger; the powers that be did not permit themselves to go to such extremes in the cities; the powers that be behaved with perfect manners in the cities, visiting the populace in black Mercedes Benzes; in the cities, pretty women received baskets of apples and grapes which the powers that be had delivered to them by soldiers rendered temporarily unfit for combat and permanently unfit for pleasure by wounds in their groins; in the cities gunshots were sometimes heard at night but that was because rats were being killed (rats were so numerous in the cities that traps alone couldn't control them); in the cities sometimes, at midnight, military trucks encircled an entire neighborhood, soldiers hammered on the doors, entered the houses, shoved aside the children who were watching them with sleepy eyes, searched every room while the officers demanded to see papers, barking out questions, always the same questions; in the cities, the powers that be saw to the security of the populace, they sent their packs of rathounds out only at night. ¶ My family must be given credit for being well informed and for remaining faithful to its opportunism. When power changed hands, my family adapted admirably to the new circumstances. ¶ The men in black, the rats who were hunted and who multiplied in the forests and then in the city's sewers, came to power. ¶ *She* can't have forgotten her mother's rush to serve the new powers that be. As soon as the men in black had installed themselves, her mother made sure that all foreign magazines were thrown onto the fire, that the foreign currency disappeared under the mattress. She took out the photos that showed her with the former powers that be, but she was superstitious enough to be afraid of ripping up pictures in which she herself appeared, so she settled for cutting out her figure and burning what was left. ¶ The men in black, toughened by years of deprivation, turned out to be less malleable than the representatives of the former decadence had been. Her mother extracted some advantages from them, succeeded in retaining certain privileges. However, she deemed the men in black a bit too rustic for her taste. Her mother would always say that manners were the principal thing. She loved torturers who could kiss a lady's hand adroitly, mass murderers who also knew how to give a lady roses, she loved men who did their dirty work out of her sight and then came back to her perfumed and dressed in white. ¶ The men in black were not given to such ceremony. Her mother grew tired of their barking, interspersed with political speeches she refused to pay attention to. She grew tired of their drab uniforms. She grew tired of the tea bags she was given, nostalgic for the fruit baskets. She grew tired of officers who no longer rode around in black chauffeur-driven cars but crossed the city crouched on rusty bicycles. Her mother saw nothing but the advantages that the new power could not give

46

her because it was much too poor to gratify her as the former powers that be had gratified her.

Faced with the question *Freedom or power?* my relatives have always chosen power; they have always chosen to be the courtiers, to align themselves with those who are implacable, to join the band of corpse tramplers. A lackey always finds another lackey ready to serve him, ready to open his mouth and receive a few crumbs of power in return. My family has always submitted with great assiduity. Because the first to subjugate themselves are also the first to be given a subordinate power. My relatives have always been the spokesmen of oppressors, the servants of butchers. ¶ As for the author of the letter written in blue ink, I am almost certain of the answer *she* would give to the question *Freedom or power?* But she is still a novice, she still has time to be contaminated by a desire for power, she still has time to rot. For the moment, she has no points of reference. She chose instinctively to keep herself at a distance. She made that choice out of fidelity to her father, the man who loathed the exercise of power but, crushed down by my family, never had the chance to opt for freedom. ¶ Does *she* want me to remind her of all this? To set her on guard against her tendency to invest in illusions? To advance the hypothesis of the cruelty, the extreme prosaicness of things? Is she expecting me to back her up in her inner struggle not to yield to facility, not to accept what is offered to her, not to get carried away? Does she expect me to light up the path that the family wants to hide from her? She says she believes in my wisdom because I have lived at the margins of life.

12

Ricin and I went to the café across the street from the D. train station. Beside us were a man in a mauve shirt and a woman with a very made-up face; when she smiles there are traces of lipstick on her teeth, and traces of powder are visible on the rolled collar of her black sweater. The man has a book in his hand. He reads a page out loud. I recognize one of Bellemort's texts:

A girl is an animal by turns docile and capricious. She seduces the men who make a show of pampering her inanity as if it were a costly bibelot. She is a blue flower who never sheds her carnivorous facade and who believes that aggressivity is proof of character. She weeps without reason, giggles over any little thing, or flies off the handle and hates without any greater judgment. She thinks that having read a few books and passed a few exams entitles her to feel a sovereign disdain for her fellow creatures and to judge them old-fashioned or ridiculous. The girl mimics the gestures of love, mouths the replies that are expected of her, then packs up her things and moves on to the setting of another story. She evokes the great love of her life in the same tone she would use to speak of the person who happens to live next door. The great love was a lodger, he moved out, another one moved in, the building has aged, and the stairs still creak under the weight of someone who walks up their flights to find a confirmation of his solitude.

Ricin says of Bellemort, He's made a name for himself with secondhand suffering. There is nothing in his work that isn't borrowed or plagiarized. He has martyrized the girls he has met only to extract their pain. Bellemort has lived on the suffering women offer up to him. He made you his assistant, the disciple who drones out his theories of disaster; at the same time you were supposed to be the doll, the pretty schizophrenic, the fruit of his copulations with a never-forgotten love of his youth. When he met eighteen-year-old you, it was as if he were meeting the daughter of the love of his youth, the daughter whose education he had neglected. ¶ All of Bellemort's women are named Encore Repetita, says Ricin. Bellemort is a Pygmalion who produces series after series of Galateas, schizophrenic pinups who neither speak nor think nor smile and whom he pins to the inside of his jacket like a veteran's medals. Bellemort's women are all alike — girls with old-fashioned souls who arrange themselves in arrogant poses, modern high-school girls who have to be snatched up before they end their trajectory in a conjugal cupboard, stuffing their skulls with the sawdust of conformity. Bellemort doesn't like women, he hates them, and he has chosen among all women the most futile specimen — the girl — only in order to hate them all the more.

Bellemort is the con artist of little souls, the comforter of crybabies and airheads, Ricin goes on; he doesn't want to hear what *I* have to say about the man under attack. Bellemort is an educator. He gives girls an antisentimental education. Here is how he describes the years I spent with him: it is the story of a master who helps his disciple realize herself before teaching her the virtues of betrayal. A man meets a girl who is like a mutilated mermaid swimming against the current and frantically struggling to put the pieces of her body back together. He wants to make an exception of her, to prepare her for a destiny different from that of women whose heavy bellies are full of bitterness. He shuts her in, protects her from the outer world. She steeps in solitude. He forbids any sentimentality. She disciplines her nature, muzzles her enthusiasms. In this way, he deprives her of herself, he performs an ablation of love on her. He knows she will betray him the day she crosses the path of a man who offers to love her without trying to educate her. He repeats to himself, When that moment comes, it will be necessary for me to accompany her in her betrayal, to guide her toward the exit. ¶ At the moment of separation, Bellemort limits himself to saying, You're leaving me to go eat out of love's hand. You look blissfully around you and expect to receive your due, your share of happiness. You talk to me about fire, you, whom I've taught to live in the ice age. You speak of your heart. But feelings . . . , everyone has them. Everyone craves marshmallows. I thought you were proud, free. And you come to me with your shoulders hunched to tell me in a tremulous voice, *He wants me.* You're like a limping animal, delighted at the prospect of being adopted. You're leaving me for a man who will give you some *ma chérie* in the morning and some *amour de ma vie* at night, who will introduce you to his colleagues while caressing your hair with one hand. You're leaving me and the world will applaud, for human beings are made in such a way that they think they'll wither up if they don't yield to facility, they believe they haven't lived if they haven't experienced the great adventure of sentiment. Remember the slogan you yourself came up with a few years ago, *Falling in love is the privilege of idiots.* ¶ At the moment of separation, Bellemort also says, I will provide you with evidence against love in general and in particular against the love you think you have for Weidman. Every day, I will have exhibits delivered to you which will demonstrate the nonexistence of that love and will ultimately persuade you that you threw yourself headlong into this adventure only because it gave you a pretext for freeing yourself from me. A disciple who doesn't betray her master is an ingrate.

13

This is not a father, it's an *idée fixe*. The men she says she
loved were the victims of this *idée fixe*. She watched them,
badgered them, molded them, thought about them until
they were nothing but a plagiarism of the father. The moment she notices that some guy has an aptitude for playing substitute father she casts her net at him, and he will
struggle in vain, she will beseech him to resemble her *idée
fixe*. As soon as this latest lover has conformed to it, she
will suspect him of only playing at being her father, she
will suspect this father of not being her true father. And
she will live in the expectation and then the certitude of
being deceived, betrayed. ¶ She used to tell me the story
of the old blind man and his granddaughter who lived
in an abandoned railway car. Back then, she looked like
a little wild thing, with skinny thighs and stringy hair,
and she couldn't be pried away from her father. To look
at them, you would have thought the father led her wher-
ever he wanted, but in fact she was the one who guided
him. He had hollow cheeks, high cheekbones, and he
wore dark glasses. She clung to his arm. They made their
way among human beings like small, silent animals, all
the more aggressive for being afraid. I remember the man
with the dark glasses and the little wild thing. She refuses
to remember. She no longer needs to cling to her father's
arm in order to move forward. Now she goes by herself. If
she falls, she picks herself up on her own. It's been several
years now since he fell and didn't get up. But that doesn't
concern her. It's no longer her business. She isn't the little
wild thing anymore. Now, she knows how to behave, she
is strong. She has forged ahead, leaving the man in the
dark glasses far behind. She loved to play the little wild
thing with him; she would put on her red checked dress

that had two pockets in front and a large bow in back. The bow was getting threadbare and the pockets were twisted out of shape, but her father liked her to dress that way. For me, she would wear her pink dress with lace, or pleated skirts. For me, she played the nice little girl with tanned legs and smooth skin. She was slyly perverse. She gave each one what he wanted. The man with the dark glasses loved the little wild thing who rode through neighborhoods perched on her bicycle. She knew how to adapt to his wishes. Meanwhile, I wanted her to be nothing more than a small star who would light the sky of my consciousness from time to time. She implemented my desires with perfect diligence: she was the distant gleam of light in the village idiot's mind. ¶ Why should I satisfy her penchant for ingratitude? She's grown tired of Illusion I; she wants novelty. She's avid for revelations, impatient to overthrow her genealogy and rewrite her history. She stamps her feet, she clamors for the portrait of the new father. And she forgets, she is already forgetting what the other one was to her for years, what the old model represented to her for so long. She no longer wants to know that he fulfilled the role of father, guide. He's a worn-out gadget that has spent too much time on the dissecting table of obsession. After a while there's nothing left. Nothing but an old skin she hangs in the cloakroom of her memories. Nothing except a not terribly flattering role as the failure, misfortune's lackey. It pleased her to imagine him, to describe him that way: humiliated, ridiculed. She cultivated this image as one fattens a rabbit in its hutch. Now, she suddenly feels like cleaning out the hutch and eating the rabbit. I'm not going to be the one who lends her a hand. She forgets. ¶ She forgets the kites he made for her out of newspaper; he used grains of cooked rice, crushed, to glue the paper together. She forgets how they used to roam the city together, on foot or on bicycles. They didn't speak to each other much. Her father's face always

looked anxious. She walked at his side, quiet. From time
to time, she raised her eyes toward him, he looked down
at her, and they smiled at each other. Perhaps she hates
me secretly because I was witness to those scenes, scenes
that prove she had a father whom she now seeks to betray; as soon as she glimpsed the chance to dream about
another father's face she leaped at it. And in what colors
will she paint this one? He'll be the seducer, the cynic, the
foreigner. The man who didn't want to encumber himself
with her. The man who pushed her out of his way. ¶ I see
them again, she and her father, hand in hand at the market. They go from stall to stall. She asks questions about
everything. She is carrying the shopping bag; it's full and
heavy but she insists on carrying it. ¶ I see them again,
digging a hole in the yard to plant a seed. For weeks, they
wait for a tree to grow in this arid soil, in this little patch
of earth. The miracle occurs. Every day when he comes
home from work, her father calls her, they kneel down
before the tree and watch it grow. I see them again, two
years later, joyous because the tree is growing quickly in
the shadow of the house, in that little corner of the yard.
¶ I see her father again in the backyard. He has bought
some wood, he is building a desk for her and painting
it sky blue, as she asked. I see her again, in the market
stall of a merchant who sells old paper. She is ten years
old. As she grew up she would become fearful, shivery,
withdrawn, but at that age she is audacious. She goes to
great lengths to get money. The father hands over his entire salary to his wife. When he wants to enjoy some slight
extravagance, cigarettes, alcohol, books, *she's* the one who
finds the money. She sells old newspapers and magazines
that the man in the dark stall buys by the kilo. I see her
in her red checked dress, perched on a little bike, a pile
of old newspapers tied on behind her. She crosses and
recrosses the city, looking for good deals. ¶ I see them
again, sitting at the kitchen table. Her father has just

bought her some pencils. He is teaching her to draw. She is clumsy but trying hard, her head bent, fingers grasping the pencil. As she struggles, her father sketches her. ¶ I see her again, in late afternoon, in front of the school where she is learning French. The street is emptying out, the students are leaving one after the other. She is waiting. She is wearing a pleated, blue checked skirt, a white blouse with a round color, little ankle socks; she is looking very polished, only her brown leather shoes are a bit worn. Across the street the vendors have closed their refreshment stand and the candy seller has folded up his booth. She is waiting for her father to come and pick her up. The street is deserted. She has been waiting for two hours. The school's facade is painted a brick red color that has a powdery surface like chalk or face paint. If you lean against this wall, the paint comes off onto your clothing, leaving red marks on the fabric. She is waiting, her school bag between her legs; she is standing up very straight. The only indication of impatience and distress is her elbow inside the white blouse; it is rubbing against the wall. She tries to scrub the red stain off her sleeve. Inadvertently, she gets some red on her cheek. She thinks about an expression she recently discovered in a dictionary, *Je fais le pied de grue. I'm cooling my heels. In the street.* She repeats it slowly, *Je fais la grue. I'm on the street, I'm a streetwalker;* she smiles to herself. When she gets home, she has red stains on her clothes and face and a strange look in her eyes. It's during the moments when her father is late picking her up after school that she begins to twist her mind into knots. At first she thinks, *He forgot me.* The next day she thinks, *I am the forgotten one.* She turns these thoughts over and over in her head. She digs through her memory for signs tending to prove that no one gives much thought to her. She remembers that the date written on her birth certificate is false: her father waited ten days before reporting her arrival in the world.

54

For ten days, she says to herself, *It's as if I didn't exist, it's as if he didn't want me. I'm the one who appeared without being seen. I'm the invisible one, the forgotten one.* In those long moments of waiting, she sowed the seeds of a drama in her head. Little by little, the suspicion came: my father is not my real father. From then on, she lived with the suspicion in her belly; she invested her capital of loss and made it grow. She expended her energy on the feeling of being forgotten.

14

I'm not afraid of the man with the dog any more now
that I know he's a shoe repairman. Ricin accuses me of
naiveté and warns me to stay on guard. Imagine him fingering the shoes, sewing them, smearing the insides with
glue—I'm sure he's a pervert, a killer. Just because he
has a mother and an occupation doesn't mean you can
assume he's harmless. ¶ The other evening, as he was
coming to knock at my door, Ricin passed the shoe repairman who was coming down the stairs with his dog
on a leash. He says to me, Make him forget you, don't go
past that shop any more, avoid that street. Your shoe repairman has the eyes of a sicko. ¶ I laugh at my former
fear, secure in my conviction that the man with the dog
is not dangerous, just lonely. To which Ricin replies, Jack
the Ripper was lonely, too; he was only looking for a little
company in the evenings. ¶ As we left the building yesterday, Ricin and I saw the shoe repairman playing sentry on
the sidewalk across the street, as usual. No one else in the
neighborhood has noticed his game. For the residents of
nearby buildings, he's just the shoe repairman, walking
his dog before closing up shop and going home. Yesterday, when he saw him, Ricin said, I'm going to speak to
him, ask him to leave you alone. ¶ I didn't have time to
hold him back. He crossed the street as soon as he had
said it and walked toward the man with the dog, who
watched him approach, then turned his back and walked
away. Ricin started to follow him but gave up. He accuses
me of deliberately seeking out exciting situations. You
want the man with the dog to be your guinea pig. You
want to know what it's like to be the shoe repairman's
doll, to be the doll of a man from your country. Don't you
see that this hothead, with his dog and the shoe leather

he spends all day caressing, is a sick man, an extremist? Don't throw yourself in his arms on the pretext that he is tracking you down, harassing you, spying on you. Take care not to become the shoe repairman's doll. If you fall into the trap he's setting for you, he'll make you into a guilty doll, he'll force you to go back to the Country, to relearn your native language, he'll put it in your head that you've betrayed the Country, that you must write in your own language. If you look to him for protection, he'll squeeze you in his arms and you'll never be able to escape. The shoe repairman doesn't represent anything to you. He obsesses you because he seems to contain a little bit of all the men you've focused your illusions on. He reminds you of your father and your uncle. He re- minds you of Bellemort, because he has the same voice — you used to laugh at Bellemort because he looked young but had an old man's voice. He reminds you of Weidman because he has the same body, the same way of walking. If you think about it a little, you'll see that he's no more than the sum total of your illusions. If you think about it a little, instead of moving toward him you will move away. You've always had to be someone's doll. With your father, you were the devoted doll, the bearable replica of your mother. With your uncle, you wanted to be perverse and mute. Then you meet Bellemort and he assigns you the task of becoming like the doll he carries inside him. For years, you read the books he has always read, you eat the food he has always eaten, you come down with the illness he has always come down with; you see to it that you are nothing more than the duplicata of his inner doll. Then you attempt a rebellion, you write the books he did not deign to write. Your friends and his look at you in astonishment — the duplicata speaks! But on closer ex- amination, their astonishment ceases; they snicker. The duplicata speaks, but does no more than reproduce the thoughts of the master. Everything is back in place in the order of things. To shatter that order, you have to get off the train. Instead of making your own way, you catch a connection, get on another moving train. You think you've escaped from yourself because the landscape is different, because Weidman's inner doll doesn't look at all like Bellemort's. With Weidman, you had a relapse, like a sick man after an operation. Weidman wanted a wife doll, a doll who listens to music. Bellemort gave you books to read and you read them. Weidman put on the music he loved and you listened. When he didn't feel like listening to music, you didn't feel like listening to music either. Even your desires were docile. With Bellemort, you were the schizophrenic doll dressed in black. With Weidman, you played the optimistic doll in colorful skirts. In love, you have always behaved like a woman in exile who hopes to fulfill all the necessary conditions in order to apply for the position of model immigrant. ¶ Bellemort ended up naturalizing you. But Weidman remained a foreign land. You never got off the boat. Deliberately, with an eye to a beautiful final fiasco, you accumulated obstacles. You had to fall for a *headhunter*, a strategist whose daily bread is the fierce battle of business, a man who has responsibilities during the day, migraines during the evening, a bad back on the weekend, and who takes vacations so he'll have time to get sick. You, the most perfect species of parasite, you, whose days spent at your writing desk remind you of the meaninglessness of your existence, you had to throw yourself into the arms of a man who is attacked, as soon as he sits down at his desk, by a frenzied pack of dogs placed there only to confirm in him the feeling of his own usefulness.

Ricin wonders what on earth I did with my days during the months in Weidman's house. I didn't do anything. I was alone until late in the evening. I used to lie fully dressed on top of the made-up bed in a bedroom with shutters I had closed. It was a way of protesting against what I saw as Weidman's betrayal. He hadn't noticed that I had discovered certain things. As soon as he left the house, I would collapse. I would lie in bed in the dark. I remembered that during my childhood I always saw Madamother lying in bed. The day after the departure of her lover, the Foreigner, she lay in bed. After that, she often claimed to be ill and kept to her bed for days at a time. I would lie in bed in the dark and think about Madamother. In the afternoon, I would get up; I couldn't let Weidman notice that I was pale. I would go into the garden. I would sit down on a chaise longue in the sun and not move until evening. Or I would go for long bicycle rides in the forest; I traveled in circles and almost never passed anyone. In the evening, when Weidman came home, I would tell him I had worked on my book. It wasn't true. I didn't talk to Weidman much; sometimes in the morning an aggressive, ironic phrase would escape me and he would go off displeased. On those days I would succeed in writing something. Listening to Madamother say, *Your father is not your real father, he only submitted to the role because you wanted to be his daughter at all costs,* I thought that Weidman had undoubtedly believed a story I was telling him, a story in which I was his only love and he was my only love. ¶ From the beginning, it hadn't rung true, as if things hadn't quite clicked into place, as if the machine had been started up before the gears were properly bolted down. I remember only disturbing details, discoveries I shouldn't have made. I became a character in a children's story. A few days ago, I read an American detective novel. The heroine sang

Let's take a walk in the woods
When the wolf's not there
  If the wolf were there
  He'd gobble us up . . .

She was going to die and she told herself that all she had dreamed of in her life was to take long walks with her father. But her father was dead, she went for a walk by herself and she met the wolf. ¶ I had arrived at Weidman's house with very little, a few books, and I had decided that the house would be my kingdom, that I would be Weidman's only love and Weidman mine . . . During the week I would stand guard over the kingdom and on Sunday we would take walks in the woods. On Sunday I went for walks by myself, during the week I no longer stood guard, I began to ransack the kingdom from end to end. There was a room in that kingdom which was used only for storage, Weidman called it Blue Beard's Chamber. I thought I would find treasures there, old toys, magic potions. I discovered a notebook. ¶ As irony would have it, during my years at school I spent a lot of time writing a thesis on the diary. I even — seriously — wrote a chapter on "The Couple and the Diary" in which I examined the discovery by the wife of the husband's diary. The whole adventure seems funny to me now, but at the time, opening Weidman's notebook, I felt as if a gun loaded with bird shot had been fired point-blank into my face. When I think about that moment, I don't see myself crying; I see my face covered with blood. I am incapable of restoring the notebook's contents for Ricin in any coherent way. I keep repeating, *In his diary, Weidman guns me down.* ¶ In connection with Weidman, I remember only strange, painful episodes. Of our trip to Italy, I remember nothing. I ransack my memory in vain, I see only this image: an obese couple. We would see them at the hotel; we called them the lovers of Verona. The man is blind, he never uses his white cane, his wife guides him; they are ugly, decked out in ugly clothes. Every evening the woman wears a new dress and each time it's a kind of enormous sack, garishly colored and bedecked with lace, which, on her, seems skimpy. They talk in loud voices, lose their

tempers for no reason, insult the hotel employees. They
go for walks in the park, in the lobby. She gives him her
arm. He mutters, his head bent toward her. He mutters.
Her only response is to caress his hair. ¶ The other image
is Weidman's face. A photo I had taken that summer,
in Verona. Several weeks after I left Weidman's house,
I went back when he wasn't there. I enter. I find some
enlargements of the photo on a table. I tell myself that
Weidman had the photo enlarged because it represents a
link between him and me, a link known only to the two of
us. I leave, taking a copy of the photo with me. That very
evening, on the telephone, I confess my theft to Weidman.
A silence follows the confession. I see Weidman again, at
his house. The next morning, I find on a desk the rough
draft of a letter. A response to a personal advertisement.
He has attached the photo to the letter, or rather, the letter has been copied out on the back of the photo. He had
the photo enlarged for this purpose alone: to present the
unknown woman in the personal ad with the gaze that I
turned toward him that summer in Verona. The draft of
the letter in my hand, I burst out laughing. I tell Ricin,
Imagine a father who wants to show slides of the family
vacation. He makes a mistake and pornographic images
flash on the screen instead. The revelation is at once so
horrible and so funny that the children shudder with a
great burst of nervous laughter.

After the discovery of the diary, I think that Weidman is
playing a double game and will continue to play a double
game for a long time. After the discovery of the diary,
I lie in wait for the enemy but fear he will abandon the
fight, give up the chance to meet me in combat. I leave
Weidman's house, but go back to see him every weekend. During the hours, the days I spend in that house,
I am on the lookout, I dread and hope to surprise the
secret plans for the war against me Weidman is girding

up for. In the slightest change—a book that isn't in its
habitual place, a photo that disappears, a post card, a
notebook, some pages blackened with his industrious
handwriting that have been added to the pile of newspapers near the bed—I see a manifestation of hostility
toward me. Weidman's house is like a battlefield the
morning after a cease-fire. The mines have not been removed. For a long time after the signing of the peace
accord, explosions still claim their victims. I advance,
guided by a mine detector; from time to time, I stumble
on a notebook, a piece of paper where some murderous
phrases concerning me are noted—and stumble is indeed the word; the explosion hollows out a crater at my
feet and I am overcome by vertigo, I fall flat on my face,
I tumble into the hole, I lie there, curled up in a ball,
and don't move. At each of these discoveries I have the
same nightmare. I am in a long, dimly lit corridor. Weidman and I are preparing for a duel, turning our backs
on each other, we pace down the corridor. A metallic
voice counts out our steps. I suddenly notice that I have
been given a cap pistol. I throw the pistol to the ground
and turn around, shrugging my shoulders, looking resigned to my defeat. Weidman puts his revolver in his
jacket pocket, comes toward me, takes me in his arms.
We move toward the door at the end of the corridor. It
opens onto a bedroom. Weidman takes off his jacket and
drapes it over the back of an armchair; he approaches me,
takes my clothes off, pulls me to the bed, lays me down
on it. Then he slips between the sheets, fully dressed,
and falls asleep. I get up without a sound, go over to the
armchair, take the revolver that is bulging out of the
pocket of his jacket. I go back to sit on the bed. It is cold
in the room, I shiver. I look at Weidman, sleeping. I put
the revolver next to his temple. Before the shot goes off,
my dream ends.

*   *   *

62

Ricin says, You're forgetting that love gives off a terrible stench. For years, under Bellemort's influence, you held back your sentimental energy, so that when you meet Weidman the dam gives away at a single blow. Your brain sets itself to manufacturing illusions — male seeking great love, female seeking sole passion, permission granted to find themselves together on small cloud, shower each other with aromatic essences. You lose, I wouldn't even say your cynicism, but your common sense. You forget that love is nothing but sweat, secretions, rancor. A simple matter of perspiration that begins in a nervous moment called *coup de foudre,* continues between sour-smelling sheets, and in the long run can only conclude in the proximity of two bad moods by day and two bad smells at night, until the final bankruptcy, the last lather, which is worked up by the fear of no longer having anyone to sweat with. The question isn't, Is the smell of love a stench or a perfume? but, What can be done to make love, which essentially stinks, smell sweeter? What can be done to banish the odor of betrayal, pettiness and falsehood that sticks to the soles of lovers' shoes just when they think they are walking on a bed of roses?

15

Strange to think that my fate, like hers, is tied to books. In this family, there is only one alternative: you go mad or you earn money. If you happen to be unable to line your pockets thickly, there is only one way out: to go mad. In this family, brains are used only for calculating, duping other people, ripping off your friends. If you're not interested in eating gold, it must be because your mind is unhinged. In this family, the fear of hereditary insanity has always been overcome by investing the family capital at a profit. Making money talk in order to silence the voices of anguish. They have always lived for this alone: to amass money, always more money, to wear diamonds on their fingers, gold around their necks, on their arms, on their ankles, to cover their dungheap with gold nuggets, to sit down on top of it and think about nothing, to keep their heads empty. ¶ In this family, no one reads; reading causes headaches, reading is unhealthy: stay away from it. In this family, the life of the mind is condemned to wither away. You do not use your head to reflect, read, look at a picture, you use your head only to calculate interest, steal money here, extract it somehow there. She and I, we chose the same way of breaking with family tradition; she made her decision under the influence of her father, who had proven incapable of bringing home anything more than a meager salary, who had never invested his money to yield a profit, who always spent the little he had in his pockets on trivialities — sometimes for himself, sometimes for her. Under her father's influence, she learned to open her eyes, to acquire money only to satisfy a whim, under the father's influence, she refused to allow them to hang gold chains around her neck and big stones on her fingers. She learned to *breathe*, she learned to let

other things into her head besides financial records. She
tied her fate to books. Tenaciously. Without knowing it,
I did the same. Books saved us, her and me. I wouldn't
have bet much on her if it hadn't been for books. And if
I hadn't drowned myself in this anarchic education, acquired without rules or rigor, I would have gone under, I
would have gone under from the first months in the asylum in Corrèze. I owe my sanity to the Monk. I didn't
speak French when I first found myself in that madhouse.
I didn't answer at all when spoken to. There was no one to
be surprised by this. I was a taciturn madman. I ended up
there thanks to the family. In the Country, it was enough
to lock me up; when I acted a little turbulent, I was put in
chains. But there was never any question of subjecting me
to a radical treatment. By sending me to that asylum, *they*
were hoping to annihilate me. Even if I wasn't destroyed,
they knew they had rid themselves of me. Being in that
asylum in Corrèze was the same thing as being dead and
buried. ¶ So there I was, a madman among madmen who
were all speaking an incomprehensible language. I had
always refused to participate in that aspect of the family
snobbery which ordained that one must know how to twitter in French. No one expected the lunatic to play social-
ite, so they had excused me from learning the language.
They achieved their goal: they isolated me, locked me up
among people who spoke a language I did not understand;
they quarantined me, marked me for death. All I could
do was waste away; I was doomed to go out of my mind.
Everything would have taken place just as they had en-
visioned it if the Monk had not appeared. The first time
I saw the Monk, I had just spent six months in a group
room—there were four of us in there. I told myself: you
must hang on, whatever the cost. I talked to myself, pre-
served my lucidity, stood guard over the wanderings of
my imagination. My defenses were beginning to weaken.
Some mornings, I neglected my regular mental exercise

which consisted of remembering every detail of the sequence of events that brought me to the doors of the asylum. But there, too, I could feel the shadows gnawing at my head, more and more my misfortune was beginning to appear to me to be the result of a plot, and in my dreams the instigators of the plot had the faces of the occupants of the other beds. Sometimes, in the evening, I let myself moan along with the others, whereas before that I had stopped up my ears so as not to hear them, chewed on a corner of the sheet so as not to cry out. I was slipping downhill. ¶ I was giving in to the urge not to struggle anymore. I was letting myself go. And then one evening, the door opened and the Monk made his appearance. His gaze slid over my roommates who were all sleeping their deep, chemically-enhanced sleep. I had the privilege of being able to fall asleep and wake up at will; I was a calm and taciturn madman and I was allowed my insomnias, I was allowed to eat my fill of hatred. The Monk's gaze fixed on me. He asked me a question. I was unable to answer him. I was seated, my face turned toward the door, my legs hanging out of the bed. I did no more than return the Monk's gaze. He had thin cheeks and a slight squint. I was particularly struck by his haircut. His hair had been shaved off very close to the scalp. Like our hair. What set the inmates apart from the attendants and the doctors was their haircut. The inmates regularly had their heads shaved, one after the other. Every two weeks, we were entitled to a few strokes of the electric razor on the tops of our heads. They pretended it was done for hygienic purposes. But there was a certain jubilation in the attendants' gazes when the black sheep were being shorn. After that, there could be no doubt: at a glance you could tell the madmen from the sane. How could you look like anything but a lunatic when your skull was naked except for a few bristling tufts of hair? The madmen no longer had a face, they were empty eggshells someone had painted a gri-

mace on. The Monk had his hair shaved short, like us.
For a moment I thought I was mistaken. That it wasn't
a doctor, but an inmate who had stolen a white jacket in
the orderlies' closet. The Monk turned around and pulled
the door shut behind him. ¶ His appearance alone was
enough, that evening, to give me hope again. I was going
to release my hold, I was preparing to sink little by little,
I was going to abdicate, to make my family right about
me. And then suddenly, a door opened, a human being
made a sign to me. Immediately I leaped up and clung to
the branch I had just let drift away. Every evening, while
my roommates slept, I sat up, face turned toward the
door; I waited. I waited until my fatigue forced me to lay
my head on the pillow. I would fall asleep like that, only
half my body on the bed, my legs hanging over the side.
After a week of waiting, I saw the door open. The Monk
had a book in his hand; it was very thick, but small, about
the size of a prayer book. He smiled. That was when I had
the idea of nicknaming him the Monk. He walked over
to me. I was seated, hands on my thighs, palms open. He
placed the book in my hands and left without a word. I
was torn between exhaustion and excitement. The exhaustion of having to begin to struggle again. The excitement
of knowing I was saved. Someone had judged me worth
the effort of saving.

The book I had in my hands was a bilingual dictionary.
I opened it and looked for how to say *Monk* in French. I
didn't look up any other word. I fell asleep, the dictionary clasped tight against me, repeating to myself this
new word I had just learned. In the following weeks, I
spent all my time reading the little book, page by page.
I always clasped it against me, even while I was asleep.
I was afraid my roommates would get hold of it. I was
afraid they would rip it from me, steal it. I listened to the
attendants with great attention. I tried to grasp the words,

to recognize them and look for their meaning in the dictionary. The little book was my talisman. The attendants' attitude toward me changed when they saw me with the book. Some of them became gentler with me, spoke to me slowly so I could memorize all the words and look up their meaning later in the book. At times I was overcome with discouragement, weeks passed without my being able to dig up a word because I could only mentally transcribe its phonetic spelling. I found a way out of this dilemma. I chose one of the attendants who was gentle with me. I repeated the word to him as I had understood it phonetically and handed him the dictionary. He opened it and showed me where the word was. From then on, I was not only concerned with memorizing the meanings of the words, I also learned how to spell them. Other attendants, however, saw my attempt to approach their civilized world as a reason to treat me rudely and even violently. They threatened to confiscate the book. I was not afraid as long as I lived under the Monk's protection. Those attendants watched me with hatred and suspicion — I was trying to blur the boundaries, I wanted to go over to the side of the normal people. They observed the Monk's behavior distrustfully; they did not understand why he had shaved his head. ¶ The Monk often came back to see me. He would sit beside me on the bed, take a pipe out of his white jacket and slowly fill it. He spoke without looking at me, the unlit pipe between his teeth. I was convinced that he was talking about himself, about a painful event in his life, but I only guessed that from his eyes, his way of remaining seated, a little hunched over, his shoulders stooped, left arm on his stomach, right elbow resting on his knee. He spoke in a firm but gentle voice, his pipe in hand. He recognized in me a man who was struggling, swimming against the current, on the verge of choking and drowning, but who continued to fight in order to keep

68

from being pushed under by the waves. The Monk had
the gaze of a man who had given up on his life.

The Monk came back to my thoughts because of a book
about a Viennese painter I paged through in the library.
H. B. draws naked bodies gnawed by patches of shadow
that are like clods of earth covering a tomb. The eyes
especially frighten me, they look like fragments of darkness. H. B.'s self-portrait gives me the same strange sen-
sation as the memory of the Monk. They both seem to
want to deceive the world around them, to offer others
a peaceful face. Their gaze betrays them. Their gaze—
their mute cry—says, Every man lives on the horror he
has seen. Their gaze says, To see is to suffer. To see is to
learn to live with a tragic shadow over your retina. I go
looking for details on H. B.'s life. I learn that in 1931,
working on a portfolio of sketches, he placed his drawing
board in the dissection room of the Saint Joseph Hospital
in Vienna. For six months, he spent every day at his pro-
visional studio, arriving and departing with the punctu-
ality of a civil servant. For six months, he recomposes the
bodies as they decompose. One evening, on his way out,
the painter finds the door of the room locked. A nurse
has accidentally locked him in. H. B. spends the night
among the dead. When he is freed early the next morning, H. B. appears to be the same man (thirty-seven years
old, married, father of a child). His eyes, though, betray a
metamorphosis. They have lost much of their light. H. B.
went into that room with the eyes of a visitor. He left with
other eyes. H. B. finally sees, finally knows. He will know
from then on that to live is to possess the ability to see
horror. There is nothing dreadful about H. B.'s cadav-
ers. They are like peaceful jellyfish. The inner film of
infamy that had attached itself to their retinas has come
to an end. The dead rediscover the innocence of the newly
born, who close their eyes, who refuse to allow the light of

the world to filter in through their eyelids. The Monk was
a man who, having survived a fire, wondered if it would
not have been better to die in the flames than to live with
his body eaten up by the burns. I was the man wandering
the borderlands between madness and lucidity. The Monk
watched me playing tightrope walker, he hesitated still:
was he going to stay there and watch me, waiting for the
moment when I would lose my balance and plunge into
madness, or would he hold his hand out to me, become
the ferryman who would conduct me to Reason? The
Monk, like H. B., had a tragic shadow over his gaze. He,
too, had undergone a metamorphosis. I didn't learn the
Monk's story until years later. Ten years to the day after
the evening when he opened the door I was sitting behind,
ready to abandon myself to despair, the Monk died and
I left the asylum. Before his death, the Monk asked the
director of the asylum to authorize my release, without
telling my family, and to find me a place to live and a job,
a job which, he specified, would leave me some time to
read. That is how I ended up soon afterwards in the room
at the Pommeraie Hotel and in the library that employs
me out of charity. ¶ In the asylum, the Monk paid me a
short visit every evening. He would bring me a few pages
torn from a book. I would read, I would look up words
in the dictionary. Sometimes it took me an entire day to
understand the meaning of a single sentence. During all
the years he was my teacher, he brought me nothing but
pieces of books. At first, he put pages from a novel or a
biography in my hands. I liked life stories, I devoured
them the way a man in quarantine devours news of the
world. Once I had acquired a more solid understanding
of the language and no longer needed to consult the dictionary for every word I read, the Monk introduced me
to poetry. Each visit, he would bring me a single poem. I
asked for more, but in vain; he laughed and said poetry
must not be allowed to render me incurable. I complained

70

that he was giving me a taste for literature but leaving me in total ignorance of all points of reference. I knew fragments of masterpieces but was unaware even of the names of their authors. The Monk advised me to cultivate my sensibility rather than stuffing my head with information. I must not pride myself, as reasonable people do, on classifying everything I had loved. From him, I learned not to label my tastes, not to behave like an erudite cop, not to organize on index cards the poems that had helped me ford the river of madness, to leave the country of madmen without entering the land of normal people. ¶ My friend gave me back a taste for living. He succeeded in getting me a room I could have to myself, in the attendants' wing. It measured nine feet by twelve feet. A closet that had been furnished for me with the bare necessities.

16

The uncle is the model—the free man, the man of passion, nobody's son, born from his own madness. The uncle whose life was saved then crushed, invented then destroyed by his love for his sister. I have an image in my head of the uncle and his sister, pressed against each other. They were afraid of the world and of the malediction the world threatened them with, but they had no fear of each other and their love. They were born for that love, and to the very end they proved themselves able to live up to that exceptional love. The uncle was his sister's only love. Her desire to nourish the feeling she had for him and watch it grow within her earned her a condemnation to death. Over the past few years, locked in his madman's cell, the uncle has lived with a dead woman for wife. All those years he struggled to safeguard his sanity because his sanity allowed him to maintain the dead woman's memory. All those years, he struggled not to yield to the temptation to put an end to his life, he struggled against himself, against his black thoughts, to keep from killing himself, because to kill himself would be to kill his love. As long as he remains alive he keeps his love alive. The uncle and his sister loved each other tremblingly: the anathema hurlers looked at them with dead-fish eyes. The uncle endured his share of the blows, but the anathema hurlers kept their mortal wound for his sister. They killed her by punishing her, denying her the uncle's presence, his body, the heat of his body. They said to her, Piece of garbage. She lowered her head. They said to her, In your veins the juices of debauchery flow. She shut her eyes. They said to her, You were born from the copulation of a swine and an idiot. She fell to her knees. They said to her, Your love will be punished by death.

On her knees, she awaited the sentence. They said to her, Piece of garbage. They said to her, Out of our sight. She was no longer any more than dust between their fingers. ¶ In their determination to safeguard themselves, to calculate the interests on their emotional investments, to loan out only forged sentiments in the hope of receiving assurances of fidelity in return — they insist on such assurances, but have no idea what the word "love" means — the anathema hurlers judged the love of the uncle for his sister indecent, indecent because there was no plan, no falsehood underlying it. The uncle and his sister shut themselves up in the little room; they read poems to each other and each lived suspended from the other's every breath. In their little room, they invented their love, knowing themselves to be condemned, she to death and he to madness. Between falsehood and death, she had chosen death. Between falsehood and madness, he had chosen madness. The anathema hurlers decreed that the uncle was mad, that he had to be cured of his bizarre love. The family sent him off for hypnotherapy, hoping he would have forgotten his obscene feelings, his unnatural love, by the time he returned. The uncle left with his little suitcase. When he refused to go off to the madhouse, his sister was locked into the little room and denied light and food. To save her, he had to agree to pass for a madman, to undergo treatment. The family lived in a constant state of alert. The uncle and his sister had to be prevented from perpetuating their crime. The uncle and his sister were watched, spied on, kept on a short leash; they had to negotiate every seclusion, every moment of conditional liberty. All day, the uncle shut himself with his sister in the little room. The family could hear the uncle and his sister laughing, talking, whispering, they could hear them reciting poems. Suddenly they heard nothing more. They imagined the two bodies intertwined. The embrace had to be torn asunder as quickly as possible, the spell had to be broken. The family erupted into the room, ordered the uncle to leave. He obeyed. He had hardly crossed the threshold when the door behind him was bolted shut, his sister was imprisoned. The uncle went back to his own room, which was almost empty because every time he was separated from his sister he would wreck the furniture as a way of demanding her release; piece by piece, all furniture had been removed, there were only a few books and a divan left. The uncle stretched out on it and remained in that position until evening without budging, refusing to go and eat his meals at the family table. He could stay that way for hours, days, starving, going over and over in his head the moments of happiness he had been able to wrest from the frenzied pack of anathema hurlers. He waited for night. ¶ When the whole house was asleep, he got up and went to scratch at his sister's door. They talked to each other all night through the door. In the early morning, the family found the uncle sleeping in the hallway, curled up in front of the door of the little room. That very day he was sent to the madhouse. He left with his little suitcase, never forgetting to slip a few books into it. When he came back, he had learned some poems by heart and was impatient for only one thing: to recite them to his sister. ¶ The love between the uncle and his sister could only lead to death. Outside their little room, they held each other back from living. Outside the little room, the uncle would go to the madhouse, then come back with his little suitcase, and throughout that time he lived without breathing. The world blew its stinking breath on him; he smelled nothing. The world sent icy air whistling into his heart but his heart had become a burning stone that kept its heat and remained out of reach. The world invited him to sample temporary loves that killed only time, loves that made the absolute just another mouthful to be swallowed. The world demanded that he let himself live but the uncle refused to let himself live,

he continued going to the madhouse, his little suitcase in hand, and then shutting himself up with his sister in the little room. The world wanted to save the uncle but there was no question of saving the sister. There had never been any question of that. She was mad herself, no doubt, because only madness could have given her the wiles by which she seduced the uncle; only madness could have sown the seeds of this demented love in her head. The world felt obliged to lead the uncle back to the straight and narrow path, but his sister, seventeen years old, was abandoned to her fate, to her unnatural love. During the uncle's absences, his sister lived confined to her room. She knew nothing of other human beings, she guessed everything from the uncle alone. No face was familiar to her, but she could draw the features of the uncle's face with her eyes closed. When the uncle was absent and she happened to escape from the room for an instant, she slipped along next to the walls, head lowered; she was silent and did not respond when the family spoke to her, not out of arrogance — she was trembling — but because out of all voices she understood only the uncle's voice. Of the world, she knew only what the uncle's eyes had seen and his mouth reported. She rejected all books except those read with the uncle. In fact, she did not read them, she only recited the passages that the uncle had read to her. She had left school years before, she deciphered the phrases with difficulty, but she had a recluse's memory: she only needed to hear a text to be able to read it immediately without stumbling over the words. She drew on her blood, her marrow, her very essence in the presence of the uncle. In the presence of his sister, the uncle drew on his blood, his marrow, his very essence. They lived in a hothouse, like barbaric flowers disdainful of all law.
¶ In the little room, they let their monstrous love grow, a love that led nowhere, that didn't allow them to dream of happiness. Would their children be beautiful? Would the

soup be warm in the evening in their home? There would be no home, never. It was a useless investment, a sterile love. The love of a madman and an orphan. From the moment this love was declared, the uncle took his sister away from the family. She was no longer anything but a bloody appendix cut off from the family's body, a piece of sacrificed flesh that twisted in pain and lived off the love the uncle gave her. When the uncle was gone, his sister was left to herself, she lay, feverish, delirious, on her bed. She waited for the uncle and the longer his absence went on, the closer death came; the fever dropped, cold took possession of her body. She was destined to live that love in the little room, to live it until she was suffocated by it, to live it like a clandestine sweetness she had torn from the jaws of guard dogs. She was condemned to disappear. No trace of her and of her love could be allowed to subsist in the family archives or in the memory of the guard dogs.

I don't remember the uncle's face, only his skinny, dejected silhouette, inseparable from the little suitcase. When he took the road to the asylum, his sister was waiting for him, seated on the edge of the bed. The memory of her is mingled with that of a painting depicting a young girl on a red divan. She is naked, sitting up straight, hands resting on her knees. She has straight hair, pointed breasts, a fixed gaze. She has just been the object of a violent act, her blood is flowing and inundates the divan with a scarlet gush. Two bluish wings shimmer in her back. When the uncle went off to the madhouse, his sister was waiting for him. Her body trembled with terror but her head was full of the poems of love she had read and recited. When the uncle went off to the madhouse, his sister shed her blood. The uncle had been torn from her. The gaping rent covered her bed with blood but in her back blue wings shimmered. ¶ She hung herself from the bars of her window. The uncle had gone off to the madhouse, his absence went on and on, the family pretended he would never return; that was the end of unnatural feelings. For whole weeks, sitting on the edge of the bed, she had waited for the uncle; he had left her a piece of clothing in which she wrapped herself at night and which rested on her knees during the day. Time passed. She waited. She kept the garment, the smell of the garment against her, her hands rubbing the fabric, which she began to rip apart slowly into strips. She placed them on the bed in a long row. Day and night she listened for the familiar step, but the uncle was slow in returning. She went back over to the bed, picked up the strips one by one, knotted them, braided them together. Then she slipped outside in the middle of the night; she picked all the flowers in the garden, took them back to the room and scattered them around the floor. The braided strips formed a long cord she tied to the bars of the window. Days went by before the family found the decomposing body. Pieces of fabric lay around the floor. The room was dark, illuminated only by a bluish light whose source no one could guess. ¶ The room was located at the end of a hallway. In the uncle's absence, no one knocked at the accursed door. In the uncle's absence, his sister never ate at the family table. At night, she slipped out to the kitchen and stole some food which she took back to her room like an animal under quarantine that must make sure its disease does not spread. The family had gotten the idea that she secreted a poison, that any contact with her was dangerous. She had to be erased from memory, buried alive in that room; she had never come into the world, never belonged to the family clan, she could not be educated, she bent her head and gave the appearance of submission but inside she was nothing but perversity because she rejected a healthy life, healthy thoughts, healthy feelings. ¶ For two whole evenings no noise came from the back room, there was no light in the window, but no one went down the hallway, no one bothered to find out if the quarantined animal was slowly dying. It was as if she had always been there, hanging from the bars of the window, as if she had always given off this unpleasant smell of outcast love, rotting flowers and decomposing corpse. ¶ The uncle and his sister had arrived at their island of love like victims of a shipwreck vomited up by the sea. They clung to each other. They spoke into each other's ears so as not to hear the voices the wind brought, which murmured to them, Love is a brief stopover, you must not give it a chance, you must not ask it for more than a seasonal diversion. The voices the wind brought also said, Love must be killed. Unleash the assassins! Give the order to take up arms and pillage the island. Let them gag all the mouths that are avid for vows. Let them crack their whips on the necks of intertwined lovers and stand them up to march in time to the rules of propriety. Let them set fire to the huts, clean the island of all feeling. Let them reestablish order. Let them ravage this land so completely that never again will a love like the one between the uncle and his sister find a place to take refuge.

17

We behave toward ourselves like comic gangsters. We
want to pull a heist on the absolute and instead we go out
unarmed to attack the convoy of petty profits. All of us
repeat to ourselves that nothing is worth experiencing
without a nostalgia for an elsewhere, but that won't pre-
vent us, meanwhile, from swiping a handful of crumbs.
We present the pitiful spectacle of those little birds who
want to fly off into the blue, but unluckily have perched
on twigs covered with gluey birdlime, so they begin to
eat the glue. We are nothing but that: glue eaters. Flying
creatures who have gotten stuck in glue and who twitter
in order to forget that they are stuck in glue. ¶ The more
glue we eat, the more our stomachs are perverted; soon
we won't tolerate any other diet. Little by little, glue takes
over our lives. We bathe in glue, we lie down at night in
glue, we read glue, our words are bubbles of glue, we pet-
rify our thoughts in glue, we spend our days kneading
glue and marshmallow—in our language, that's called
feelings. And finally, we request that flowers of glue be
planted on our tombs in tribute to the faithful servants
of glue that we were. ¶ All my life, the Monk said just before dying, I've abused the right to glue myself down. I
knew I was nothing more than a little ball of glue that you
could stick here, then pry up and stick somewhere else.
Knowing that didn't give me any advantage at all—I fell
into the category of glue ruminators I ate glue in perfect
lucidity. I watched myself sink into the glue, but nothing could turn me away from the glue pot. And when I
leave this world I'll take my glue-soled shoes with me.
¶ Ten years to the day after the evening he opened the
door I was seated behind, the Monk died and I left the
asylum. The Monk died alone. I had always known him to

be alone, never leaving the confines of the asylum, sleeping on a cot in his office. It was the solitude of a ball of glue that turns in on itself, no longer adhesive, not sticking anywhere and waiting to disintegrate. After arriving at that asylum in Corrèze, the Monk never again saw the woman he had married twenty years before. (In youth, out of ambition, you dream of marriage as a potion that will allow you to forget love and enable you to think about other things, the Monk said. The essential thing is to find a mate with whom to share the glue pot. After that, it's enough to clutch each other, cling to each other. Once you've gotten into the habit, you go nowhere without taking along the glue-soled shoes that will always bring you back to your initial error.) The Monk had arrived one day in the asylum in Corrèze, installed a cot in his office, and never again crossed the threshold of the hospital. He brought along some books, which he read until late in the night. The Monk had the look of a man fleeing from his own ghost. He had fled the big city, the woman he had married twenty years before, the hospital of which he was the director, to end up in that asylum in Corrèze. He decamped. (Of all the powers a human being possesses, the Monk had said, the power of decamping is the one we resort to with the greatest frequency: we spend all our lives gluing ourselves down and when the occasion arises to unglue ourselves we decamp, but always taking our glue-soled shoes with us.) The Monk decamped because of the specter of a young woman. She was twenty years old. She had entered the Monk's clinic after having spent most of her life in hospitals and nursing homes. She no longer had a name. She was Sleep Flower. She slept and did not speak; when she awoke, she couldn't make up her mind to get out of bed and dandled her head when she was forced to stand up. When it was time to go for a walk, she inched along, bent forward, her shoulders hunched, her eyelids half closed; she clung to the orderly's arm, then let herself slip and in an instant fell to the ground, an inanimate mass. She had to be carried back to her bed where she slept for long hours at a time. She would always awaken with a start. She sat straight up in bed and opened her mouth as if she were making a tremendous effort to speak, but no sound emerged; her face twisted into a painful grimace but she was unable to pronounce a single word. She produced only hiccups, then, out of discouragement, fell back to sleep.

There is nothing more loathsome, the Monk had said, than a man who has hidden from himself, who manages his life as if it were an inherited business, merely renewing the stock occasionally and taking inventory at the end of the year. I would never have moved my little finger to disrupt that loathsome life. My days were loathsome, my certainty of my own usefulness was loathsome, the feelings I had for my wife were loathsome, loathsome the presence at my side of that dried-up plant who had, through the position I occupied, a loathsome consciousness of the place she was entitled to on the merry-go-round; also loathsome was my insistence on faking deafness, not listening to the little voice that, in moments of silence and solitude, told me I had let myself go, that I was getting ahead by forgetting myself. When did I lose track of myself? A dream often came back to me. I'm looking for an address. In the distance, a sign glows. I go toward it. Above the heavy door pierced by a metal grating I read the number: oo—the same number written on the piece of paper in my hand, and the neon letters, *All born of unknown father*. A face was silhouetted behind the grating. I fled. Behind the heavy wooden door lay aborted urges, pillaged loves, rejected desires. It was the boutique of eternal regrets. ¶ I had to keep myself away from that door, to remain the customer of my loathsome life, to close my eyes during the day and open them only

at night to stare at the double zero, those two round num-
bers, smooth and perfect in their nullity. I was a plucked
bird nesting on rotten eggs, a bony old man with nothing between his legs any more but pouches of vomit. The
little voice whispered *All born of unknown father* to me
but I refused to push open the door of eternal regrets.
¶ Once again I sought refuge in books. Thanks to books
I had been able to come to an arrangement with myself,
choke back my disgust. Books had saved me. And it was
a book that lost me. I read this fragment in the diary of a
philosopher: A drunken man wanders the streets with his
drinking companions, they walk past a woman, undoubtedly a prostitute, the man spends part of the night with
her. His companions take him home. The next morning,
he doesn't remember a single detail of the night, but he
awakens with the certainty that during those few hours
he became a father. In the days and weeks that follow
he looks for traces of the prostitute. In vain. The years
pass, the man does not marry, he lives alone, when he goes
out his feet always take him toward the streets of ill re-
pute. He looks in the faces of the children he passes and
finds in some of them a certain resemblance to himself.
¶ I closed the philosopher's diary. A face appeared to me
clearly, the face of a young woman with large black eyes,
behind the window of a train station buffet — I searched
for the name of that city in the north, but everything had
been swallowed up by the glue pot. Only the trace of a
night, twenty years before, spent in a hotel near the train
station in that city in the north, and the memory of a
mass of hair with the scent of tea and large black eyes set
in a very pale face. The large black eyes were dry. They
watched me without expectation, without illusion. They
knew me for a glue eater. I promised myself not to forget the name of that city in the north, to go back there
and find the woman who never wept, who said she had
never wept. The large black eyes watched me through

the window of the train station buffet. I got back on the train. I went back to the wife I had just married, who was unable to give me a child. I plunged back into the glue. Everything else was swallowed up.

The dream of the double zero came back. Behind the metal grillwork, the large black eyes stared at me. But a glue eater learns above all not to be afraid of dreams. I forbade myself to stock up on the eternal regrets in the double-zero boutique. I forbade myself to remember the name of the city in the north and the face of the woman who never wept. I forbade myself to stare at the faces of children in public parks, trying to recognize my own. I had one task to accomplish. For twenty years, I had been taking care of madmen, buffing their skin, making them clean, docile; for twenty years I had been showing them the shortest route to the glue pot. ¶ Sleep Flower had been given to me for that purpose. I was supposed to find some toeholds for her, to guide her toward the glue pot. She slept; she needed to be taught how to glue herself down. She had arrived at the clinic a few days before. From my office window, I had seen her walking in the park, her shoulders hunched, her chest leaning forward. I said to myself with disgust that she didn't deserve the name she'd been given; she looked more like an insect than a flower. ¶ Throughout the week, I found pretexts for not going to see her. Then one afternoon, I slipped into her room, alone. The bed beside hers was empty. Sunlight filled the room. Sleep Flower was sleeping, the blankets pushed to her feet. Her disheveled hair hid her face. Curled up, enveloped in her immaculate gown which left her milk white legs uncovered, she made me think of a dead cockroach that had rolled in plaster. I did not wake her up. I stood at the foot of her bed. I waited. She slept without a sound. Her breathing was barely percep- tible. ¶ She woke up with a start. I saw her sit up in bed,

eyes wide open. In terror, she stared at the strange man
who had entered her room while she slept. I took one
step back. Two large black eyes were staring at me. Sleep
Flower opened her mouth, her face twisted into a grimace. I fled from the room. I shut myself in my office and
did not come out until nightfall. I had asked to see Sleep
Flower's records. On the first page appeared the notice,
Born at B. of unknown father. I left the hospital, knowing I would never go back. The door of eternal regrets
had opened, the woman with large black eyes was coming
toward me. I had returned to the point of departure: oo.
A month later, I arrived in Corrèze. ¶ On a winter night,
a man paces back and forth in front of the fireplace in
his bedroom. He is alone. He is inside where it's warm,
but he is alone. He tells himself that outside there may
be men wandering, cold and alone. He throws another log
onto the fire, picks up his coat—he must save the men
he imagines shivering in the night . . . Early in the morning he returns, worn out, alone. In front of the door of
his house, he trips on an inert mass. It's the corpse of a
woman, frozen to death. The man steps over the body,
enters his home, locks himself in his bedroom and kills
himself. That's my whole story, the Monk said. I would
have had to save her or kill myself. But I had eaten too
much glue. I ran away.

18

When the uncle came back from the madhouse, the back
bedroom was empty, the door boarded up. The body of
the hanged woman had been buried in a cemetery far
from the city; the books and the few clothes she had were
burned at the far end of the garden. The uncle came back,
his little suitcase in hand. There was no longer any trace
of his sister. The family had cleared the ground, puri-
fied the air, chased away the foul odor of unnatural love.
Access to the back room was forbidden. The uncle set his
little suitcase down in front of the door and sat down on
the ground, head between his legs. For three days and
three nights he remained in that position; on the morning of the fourth day, his body listed, he fell to one side,
inert. The family had him taken back to the madhouse.
The little suitcase was left in front of the door. After the
uncle's departure, the hallway that led to the back room
resounded for a whole night with a monotonous voice, a
solitary voice that sometimes hummed, sometimes recited inaudible texts. Then the voice was silent. A smell
of rotten flowers filled the corridor, permeated the walls.
Around the house, the garden no longer bore flowers. The
family said that the dead woman tore off the flowers, that
she ate them, that she scattered them on the floor of the
empty room to make a bed for herself. ¶ The family also
said that the death of the uncle's lover was a small misfortune, the epilogue to a great misfortune (the love the
uncle felt for his sister), the incident that would make
it possible to control the damage that had been done,
to erase the proofs of the uncle's madness. If only the
hanged woman would not show such arrogance, if only
she would not return to persecute the living with the
smell of rotting flowers . . .

*   *   *

Of the uncle and his sister there remained only that smell
of decomposition and the little suitcase that no one had
moved from its place in front of the door. The lover with
her rotting flowers was crossed out of the family's memory, the man with the little suitcase was sent off in an
airplane several weeks later in the direction of an asylum
in Corrèze.

I rediscovered the lover with the rotting flowers in the
features of an American actress who has a child's body,
stooped shoulders, long, tousled hair, a small mouth,
frightened eyes—it is the broken lily who takes refuge at
the side of the man with the suitcase. They stand pressed
tightly against each other like migrant workers who have
been chased away with stones; they don't know where to
go so they stay at the edge of the sidewalk. They cover
over the wounds they bear with a vehement silence. Im-
placably they watch the world that has stoned them, mutilated them. They close their fists; they are waiting for the
cortege of the absolute that will carry them away, far from
this world that hustles and bustles and rusts.

19

I don't know why, but lately I've started to think that she's very close to me, as only one other person has been close to me, and at the same time that she is my enemy. She wants to make use of me, she wants to steal the baggage of my life. If I don't watch out, she will strip me of everything, my love, the Monk, my years in the asylum, the days spent here in the Pommeraie Hotel. She is my enemy because there can't be two escapees in this family. In my own way, I got away from them. I know that from now on I am out of their reach. *They* can no longer do anything to me but she may lose her skin, if not her head, in this business. They still have the power to resuscitate the genetic links, to torture her spirit until she's no more than a rag doll in their hands. Perhaps she foresees this. So she wants to make me her ally. I can't do anything for her. I refuse to show her the way. I don't know any way to show her. All I did was sit down at the side of the road; I watch all the people whose ecstatic eyes gaze fixedly at a goal—but when I look in the same direction, all I see is a light mist. She, too, she is running down that road, but she recognized me, she would like to know why I'm not running: if I'm sitting here watching the others pass by it must mean that there is something interesting here beside the road. She wonders if I am wise or sick, if I've decided to give up running or if I fell and can't pick myself up. All the questions she's dreaming up, it's only because she thinks it's *interesting* to wonder about them. It excites her mind. It makes the inside of her head sizzle. She likes to put her gray matter to work. That's how they'll get to her. She is still young, she's ready for every experience (precisely because she believes that they are no more than experiences). The revelation of her illegitimacy was, to her, another interesting experience, the realization of an old dream. Immediately she wants to have all the details, even if some of them have to be invented. She will always demand more interesting experiences. There will be dead bodies along the way, but she won't count them. Her mind will start to warp, but she'll think she is ushering life into her brain. ¶ She tells me that she has broken off all ties with the family. She's no longer anything but a body amputated from its limbs, she has learned to live that way, to go on alone, to reject anything that smells of blood ties. She tells me that for all these years she has disciplined her memory so that the family's flaws will not come back to haunt her. She tells me she is cured of the family, that she has expelled all the germs from her body, that she has scoured her soul clean, that she has purged the bitter humors from her head. For her, the family was a childhood illness, improperly treated, whose aftermath spoiled years of her youth. Her mother noticed that she was seceding from the family, and that even if it meant rotting away she would rather fall apart by her own fault, of her own will, on her own, far from the family. Her mother noticed that she wanted to keep to herself. But in this family only the one who finds himself in an asylum is authorized to keep to himself. In this family, the only place you can play by yourself is in the shadow of the deadly nightshade. She thought she had sweated out the poison. She thought she had come out of it safe and sound. How could she imagine she would succumb to them again so easily? Her mother found a way of digging her claws back into her by giving her an exclusive on this *love affair*, an impossible *histoire d'amour* between an officer of the occupying army and a disillusioned young wife. ¶ She tells me that during all the years when she had withdrawn from the family, all the years when she put her childhood memories in quarantine, she always thought of me, she always felt great kinship with me, she lived very close to my madness. She says she never believed I was ill. She pretends to know instinctively what madness is, what my life has been like. She believes she lives at the margins of the normal world, she thinks she is already off balance. She is deceiving herself. There's a long distance between the vertigos experienced by the potential lunatic and the fall to the bottom of the hole. The one on whom the doors of the asylum have closed lives in a hole and will try to crawl out in vain. He fights to preserve his reason, sharpen his lucidity, but he isn't duped; he knows he's out of the running. He saves face by playing the little chieftain among the toy soldiers. ¶ Somehow, I must get these subtleties into the head of that pretentious woman. She wants to be the heiress of my sorrows, the legatee of my vertigos. There is no common measure between what she has learned or intuited and the horror that has been the color of my days. She dreams that she is close to me, but she's deceiving herself. I'm no more to her than *an interesting character*. All the other members of the family have hushed their madness by leading pallid lives, they wanted to dominate their madness, in the hope that a conventional decor, an ultraconformist lifestyle would save them from the catastrophe. Only she and I have in some way tempted the devil. I fell off balance. She saw the time and the place where I went down. She sidestepped the hole. She says she wants to make something of her madness but in fact she wants to make something of *my* madness. I'm not going to let her dispossess me of it.

It suits me quite well to have ended up as the family's official spokesman. My mouth will speak the insanities of that band of crazies. That tribe of sick-in-the-heads will be identified with my nightmares. The family's rot will be apparent in my smell. ¶ Only madness could save me from the hereditary immorality. Only madness could spare me the petty sins and the petty-bourgeois lusts that are the family's lot. They transgress, but quake while doing so. The fear of consequences has always been with them. Meanwhile, my life has been a long solitary confinement; sex has been a delirium or a feeling of disgust. A delirium in the night, moans that were not echoed, convulsions not provoked by contact with any body. The disgust of dirty sheets, bodies torn apart, penetrated by the dream's savagery. And when the sheet is lifted, nothing but the trace of a solitary disorder. In the morning, I hear the orderlies making fun, The Chinaman's beauty came to him in the night, then she left, and no one saw her!

20

Ricin says, Before they are human, women are falsehoods
that live and flourish. ¶ It sometimes happens that Ricin
disappears for three weeks or a month; he lets the phone
ring, doesn't answer the letters slipped under the door
of the two-room apartment that serves as the office of
his publishing house. Then he reappears one evening in
front of my door, his eyes reddened, holding his cigarette
in a shaky hand. I get my coat, a book. I follow him. We
walk through the streets without speaking. He sometimes
stops to make a call at a pay phone. We wind up in a café
and while waiting for the waiter to bring him his glass of
wine, he goes downstairs to call again. His calls last half
an hour, an hour; he comes back up to change a bill at the
counter. He seems to have forgotten my existence. I watch
him coming and going. I read, drinking water. Finally he
comes back, falls heavily onto the banquette, throws his
head back and murmurs his favorite poem,

Under the spreading chestnut tree
I sold you and you sold me.

When Ricin recites these lines, I know he has settled matters once and for all, taken inventory of the past three
weeks and closed the door on the new lie. Life resumes its
course. The next day, Ricin comes knocking at my door,
we go for a walk, he talks to me about what kept him away
for those three weeks, he vomits out his spite. Ricin ar-
ranges things so as not to have to live through long love
stories, only brief stories of betrayal. He does not seek
the woman of his dreams, he tracks down the reflection
of what he hates—*My mother is dead and I'm glad. From
now on I'm going to hate all women.* Toward women, Ricin
has the attitude of a terrorist toward superpowers: he goes

to them and infiltrates their lives for the sole purpose of humiliating them, wounding them, leaving his mark on them. What attracts him to them is his own desire to destroy them, to annihilate them. And like a terrorist, he invokes an ideal of purity: he wants to return women to their initial candor. He thinks he loves them, but he trails them in order to massacre them. He drugs them on his presence, his insults, he crumples up their pride, hands them a mirror and tells them again and again that they are nothing but vanity and rot, then abandons them in the certainty of having been betrayed by them. ¶ He says, Most men behave like pimps toward their wives. They protect them and are contemptuous of them. The wives are nothing more than their toy, their doll, in the best of cases their victim, in the worst the accomplice who gives them the stepladder that lets them into the homes of the rich, and once they have set foot there they make the wife come in behind them like a dog. But he, Ricin, behaves toward women like a cop or a priest who missed his true vocation, which was to be a pimp. He intends to reform them, he indoctrinates them, he leads them to the recognition that they prostitute themselves only in order to satisfy their vanity. He demands that they acknowledge their own futility, their frivolity. Once they have performed their self-criticism for him, he sneers and takes off with a slam of the door. The dream of all women, he says, is to find themselves on trial in order to proclaim their own innocence, in other words, in order to lie in front of a large audience. ¶ Ricin hunts down the reflection of what he hates: the young woman who lives alone, pretends to care only about her career and her independence, cultivates a certain sentimental disorder, wears short skirts, smokes blond cigarettes, goes home very late, and falls asleep without having removed her makeup. He says, I feel a desire for their body, but their face repels me. I want to rip voluptuous cries from them as long as they shut up afterwards. As long as they leave me alone, as long as they don't sprawl back on the bed with satisfied face and moist cunt to smoke a cigarette while spouting off a lot of bullshit about their inner life. If they would only spare me their minute of vulnerability. I know what attracts them to me: their collection is lacking a confirmed loser, a dog that barks at every caravan that rolls by. Women think that devotion is the pitying gaze they give those who don't live up to their ambitions. Women always have a weakness for burdens and dead weights. Often in the evening, I think about tying myself to my chair. I stop my ears. I hold my own weakness against myself. I repeat to myself, Lock yourself up. Hide yourself in your bed, under your sheets. Endure your solitude. Don't go begging them for another embrace. They flutter in front of your eyes, they follow each other in quick succession, they are all named Disaster, they don't bring you the slightest happiness, they want you because you act like you are rejecting them though ultimately no one needs them more than you do. You need to crush your fingers against their lips, need to feel their flesh tear apart, need to do violence to them. You know there is no tenderness, that the whole thing is a matter of bed, sweat, and disgust. You take them the way a soldier picks up a live grenade. With the same fever, the same horror. ¶ Ricin is telling himself stories. The years go by and the grenade is no longer charged with any explosives. Ricin needs women the way other people need narcotics — taken at night, they leave no trace the next morning, and the secondary effects are the same as well: habituation and memory loss.

21

When I compare life in the Pommeraie Hotel to the life of normal people, one image always comes back: I see the people outside as vacationers cruising by in a boat while we are survivors hanging on to this place as if it were a dead branch, and I wonder why we cling to it since we are doomed to drown in any case and sooner or later we will let go. ¶ A few days ago, coming back from the library, I found a hearse in front of the building. Two men in gray were taking a coffin out of it. They entered the building. I went through the door after them. In front of the elevator an old couple were standing; they live here. The man is Turkish, the woman German. They are holding each other tightly, and clutched together like that they look even thinner, even tinier than they really are. They are wearing clothes that must have been black a few years ago and that are now the color of rotting wood. With the back of her hand, the woman wipes the tears that are pouring out, inundating her face framed with beautiful white hair cut short. The man is standing up very straight, he does not weep. His eyes slide over me, move toward the men in gray, stop at the coffin. He lets out a brief laugh. The woman grasps his arm, squeezes it. He laughs harder. His laughter resonates in the lobby, he laughs like a guest who has been told an off-color after-dinner anecdote. I rush to the stairs, where people from the building have started to gather; I climb the stairs four at a time and lock myself into my room. Since that incident, I think I hear bursts of laughter that wake me up in the night.

Two red buildings facing each other make up the Pommeraie Hotel. Between the two buildings lies a lawn, and from the window of an upper floor one can watch the comings and goings between the buildings. One night, I wake up with violent pains in my head. I switch on the light, look at the clock over the bed: three A.M. I'm no longer sleepy. I pick up the book lying on the night table. I read. The words dance. I feel dizzy. I turn off the light and get up. I go smoke a cigarette near the window. There is frost on the glass. I am standing in the dark. I look down at the lawn below, lit up by streetlamps. I see the front door of the opposite building open. A silhouette slips outside. A very thin silhouette walking with rapid steps. She is enveloped in a white coat with a hood that hides her face. She crosses her arms over her chest, her coat is unbuttoned. Her copper-colored legs are bare. She has on little shoes without heels, ballerina flats. She walks quickly, shivering under her coat, she crosses the lawn without lifting her eyes; she wants to hide her face under the hood. Then she disappears from sight. I hear the noise of the elevator, which stops at one of the lower floors—perhaps the third floor. The following night, I wake up at the same hour. I stand in the dark, on the lookout behind my window. The front door of the opposite building opens. A silhouette slips out. A little elf crosses the lawn in her thin white coat. ¶ During the day, I begin to look around me, trying to find the white coat. Most of the women I walk past are overflowing with fat, a few are slender, but they are also tall and wear high heels and close-fitting coats. Every night, I watch the white butterfly flutter across the lawn. Then she disappears until the next night. I'm tempted to run out, leap down the stairs and go to meet her. I remain glued to my window, watching the ballerina flats graze the wet grass. In the morning, I carry on with my investigation. For nothing. I don't dare speak to the adults. I mingle with the groups of children, I ask them if they've ever played with a little girl wearing a white hooded coat. They laugh, hide, or shake their heads. No one knows who the little elf in the white hooded coat is. I'm beginning to believe that solitude and insatiable desires are making me see ghosts. ¶ One evening I go back to the Pommeraie in the rain, I'm wet, water is running down my face. In front of me, a white form walks very quickly in the direction of the red buildings, a thin form, scurrying along, which seems to be carrying a very heavy weight, a shopping bag. I break into a run, pursuing the silhouette in the white hooded coat. I come up next to it, catch my breath, stretch out my hand and push down the hood of the coat. I recognize the young boy from Madagascar who lives on the third floor. He is a quiet boy, ten, maybe twelve years old. I once asked him if he knew of a girl in the building who wore a white coat, and he turned on his heels and went home without a word. ¶ We stand there face to face under the rain, thunderstruck. He is carrying a very heavy bag filled with bottles of liquor and wine. I grab his shoulder. That coat isn't yours. He avoids my gaze, turns his head toward the Pommeraie as if hoping for help. Water falls on his curly hair. Suddenly he jerks away from me and puts the hood back on his head. He says, It's my sister's, before moving off. The phrase leaves me speechless for a moment. I get a grip on myself, I run, catch up to him. I blurt out, I want to speak to your sister. He doesn't answer, he walks, without lifting his head, as quickly as the weight he is carrying allows—I hear the bottles clinking against each other. He says, She isn't allowed to go out because she has to work at night. We are approaching the lawn that separates the two buildings, the lawn the white butterfly drifts over every night. The boy lifts his eyes toward the building's windows. He jumps; I feel the fear that makes his thin body quiver under the coat. I peer up at the windows. Behind one of them, on the third floor, a heavyset man in an undershirt is standing. I've passed him in the building. He doesn't work and often comes home fairly drunk. I have stood in front of him in the elevator. His body exudes a smell of alcohol, sweat, and vomit. From his window, the man watches us. The young boy quickens his steps, but I still want to ask him a question. He turns around and says, nodding toward the man in the window, If you want her to come to your place tonight, you'll have to ask *him*. ¶ One of the Pommeraie's tenants is getting married. He is having a party in the big dining room on the ground floor. On weekdays, the smells of fried fish and potatoes drift up to the floors above. Holidays are recognizable by the smells of fritters and grilled sausages. All the residents of the building are invited, if the large sign on the elevator door is to be believed, but some of them know it's best not to expose themselves to the humiliation of having to beat a hasty retreat after seeing themselves cast as the undesirable guest. I owe it to normal people, happy people, not to offend them with my presence. My personal pleasure is to depart from the duty normal people assign me, to spoil their pretensions to happiness; it is my pleasure to show my ugly mug like a bird of ill omen come to croak in the midst of their rejoicings. With a spring in my step, I enter the room. It is filled entirely with women. Women with heavily made-up eyes and painted lips, planted on patent leather shoes with worn-down heels. The eldest of them are sitting on chairs. The others are scattered around the room. There are two negresses, one of them obese, with a laughing face, enveloped in a blood-red shawl, the other thin, dressed all in black, circling near her mother like a frightened mosquito; the rest are from the Maghreb. Pushed against the rear wall, two bare tables are awaiting their food. A group of little girls in scarlet dresses comes out of the kitchen holding steaming hot fritters in their fingertips; they rip them in half to extract the piece of banana which they wolf down, then they savor the oil-soaked dough, their heads thrown back, giving little bursts of laughter. The gaze the women turn on me tells me that their pleasure is ruined, that the evening promises to turn into a catastrophe because the first man to appear before them was the lunatic from the fifth floor. I glance over the room, hoping to see a hooded coat, but the white butterfly isn't there. I smile at the black woman in the red shawl and turn on my heel. ¶ I brought back from the library a book taken out of the philosophy section. As I leafed through it, a sentence caught my eye. *It is no fun to play in a world where everyone cheats, beginning with me.* Perhaps I won't read this book all the way through, maybe I won't read it at all; it is enough for me to know that I've had it in my pocket, there close against me, in the right hand pocket of my jacket, the book that contains these few words. *It is no fun to play in a world where everyone cheats.* I don't read out of a desire for erudition. I look in books for a sign of recognition. I leaf through a lot of them. Most of the time, I see nothing other than a book, some paragraphs, some words. I get tired of turning the pages. I'm ready to stop. Then the miracle happens. I pick up a book, I open it, and something there makes a sign to me. In those moments, I feel like a shipwrecked man who sees a hand on the horizon, a hand waving on the surface of the water, a living hand. A hand that can do nothing for me. But still, a hand that signals to me, tells me that at least there are two of us shipwrecked here in this sea of solitude. When a book makes a sign like that to me, I carry it back to my room, I set it on the table next to my bed. Suddenly, the room is inhabited, inhabited by a master who confides to me, *It is no fun to play in a world where everyone cheats, beginning with me.* I mull over this phrase—there's enough there to feed on for days, weeks. At other times, I take the book with me, I keep it in my pocket. It keeps me warm. It's like a friend whom I meet for the first time every morning. I introduce myself to it, *I'm a stranger here.* It answers me, *Je ne suis pas d'ici non plus.* We turn our back on the world, we walk in the same direction, we set out to conquer the great Nowhere.

On the wardrobe in my room, I've just put up a photo I found in a library book; I ripped out the page, slipped it under my shirt and went home. The woman in the photo is named Käthe K., she is German, she does drawings and sculptures. Two books that are in the library have been written about her. For a few days now, I've been leafing through books on art. Most of Käthe K.'s drawings show a mother who is defending her children against Death and finds herself swallowed up by the Great Shadow. It wasn't the drawings, but Käthe K.'s face that caught my eye. In the photo, she is about sixty years old. Her white hair, which seems smooth and soft, is pulled up into a chignon. She has a pointed face, barely wrinkled at all, she looks like a little white mouse. When I stand in front of the wardrobe facing her, I feel as if her right eye is staring at me while her left eye tries to make out another presence behind me. Käthe K. watches me, half-madwoman, half-monk. She is the guardian angel of the Pommeraie Hotel. She defends me against death, against madness. She watches over my sleep. The room doesn't seem as cold now, even the metal wardrobe seems to give off some warmth.

22

The Counselor's office smells of ambush. I enter the bare-walled room with its disparate pieces of furniture like an emissary entering the chamber where a peace conference doomed to certain failure is being held. The Counselor receives his visitors seated in an armchair behind a large table loaded down with files. In fact, the Counselor doesn't receive; he confronts the witness with his ugliness, he prepares to spit in the mirror that shows him his image. There is nothing monstrous about the Counselor's ugliness, no hint of deformity. It is dull, unimaginative, merely disagreeable to look at. As if, on a whim, the prop master decided to select from his stock whatever was most insignificant, most morose, to include in the Counselor's face: thick, gray skin, a piece of flesh awkwardly whittled to the size of a nose and stuck in the middle of the face, two narrow strips forming a sort of beak below it, small eyes barely visible behind the slit of the eyelids, and heavy, pendulous cheeks that make the Counselor look like a bulldog, one of the finest specimens of that acrimonious canine breed. The Counselor thinks to hide his ugliness behind an arrogant pugnacity. He has one thing to say: Take it or leave it. One doesn't know if the ultimatum concerns the Counselor's unprepossessing physiognomy or the business at hand. The Counselor speaks in a dry voice, breathes quickly, makes up his mind in a flash. His sharp mind is constantly on the alert for what must be thought, said, read, written, produced, *launched.* He has no personal opinions. Depending on the interlocutor sitting across from him, he justifies himself with cynicism (personal opinions bring you nothing but troubles and insomnia; I have a horror of *idées fixes,* I prefer to cultivate my mental agility—I am *as fast as the*

passage from good to evil) or with feigned humility (when
he compares himself to an echo chamber, to the Nurem-
berg funnel once used to pour knowledge down children's
throats: the Counselor seeks to become the funnel that
gathers together all the loose opinions fluttering around
and force-feeds them to the public). He says his person
is of no importance, what he thinks isn't worth a sou. He
runs after the ideas of another, the urges of another. This
other: who is he? The Counselor doesn't know, but his
function is to think like *the other.* On any subject at all,
he is capable of carrying on two separate discourses. I've
heard him say, There is no such thing as love, only pity for
the animal who, like you, walks through the streets saying
over and over, *If only I won't be alone tonight.* Remind him
of his function and the Counselor instantly sloughs off his
cynicism and spouts commonplaces in a tone that is both
definite and affected. No sooner has the Counselor sur-
feited his interlocutor with a long discourse (which con-
cludes with a sonorous, I'm not asking you to sell me your
soul, I'm asking you to give me a product), then he pulls
back inside his shell. He pushes his little round glasses
up his nose and straightens his shoulders, making a face.
He believes he has won the battle. He stands up, certain
of his victory. He doesn't know that at the very moment
he believes he has triumphed, his body betrays him — as
if he had worn his strategy on his face and let the rest of
himself go. He has the face of a strategist and the body
of a conquered man. When he leaves his seat, the body
that appears is flaccid, round-bellied; a certain languor
in its gestures contradicts the energetic expression of the
face. The Counselor has worked on that expression, has
given himself the jaws of a predator, eyes with daggers
rolling in them, but once he has won the match he takes
refuge, unwatched, in his soft, warm body. Ricin tells me,
When you find yourself across from the Counselor, try

not to look at his body or he will end up making you feel sorry for him. Concentrate your attention on his face. You can read his one desire there: war. War makes him forget his ugliness. In war, there is no such thing as a man, a woman, and unequal chances: in war there is nothing but two enemies and a ton of explosives. The Counselor machine-guns you with his intelligence and his contempt. His intelligence isn't sure of itself, his contempt is only an anticipation of the contempt he fears being the object of. Ricin says, You must throw acid in his face, shower him with insults. He doesn't want your pity. He wants to be your adversary. ¶ In the Counselor's office, to the right of the door, a bookshelf runs the length of the wall. On it, he has placed his collection of hands. For years, the Counselor has collected hands. This passion undoubtedly came to him the day he noticed an oddity in his makeup: one element escaped from the general ugliness. The Counselor has beautiful white hands, with long, delicate fingers. The prop master played a mean trick and gave him the hands of a seminary student. The Counselor's hands do not seem alive to me. Looking at them, I imagine that he cut off his hands and grafted on casts of the hands that he collects. I imagine that the Counselor changes hands as one changes gloves, that each morning he fastens plaster hands or hands cast in bronze to his wrists, depending on the visitor he is expecting. When the visitor is me, he wears white hands. When he joins them together in front of his mouth, as if in prayer, I think of butterflies whose wings have just been snatched by the jaws of a mastiff. The Counselor likes to show me his hand collection, hands of all dimensions, in every material, a bronze cast of a pair of extraordinarily delicate female hands, small hands made of pink marble, robust hands, a strangler's hands in steel, or wooden hands, whose joints, threaded together on a string, can be detached from each other.

Above the hand collection, the Counselor has hung an advertisement for a brand of perfume showing a model with blond hair wearing a dark green suit—her hands can't be seen in the picture, only laughing blue eyes and a mouth with scarlet lips. The picture is like a job announcement addressed to the women who enter the office. The Counselor has the weakness to advertise his tastes, but he doesn't expose himself to the ridicule of setting out to conquer his dreams. He fears humiliations. He detests failures. He makes do with what he has on hand. What he has on hand is called Mademoiselle Monnier. The idea was born in the Counselor's mind the day Mademoiselle Monnier applied for the position of assistant which he was seeking to fill. The Counselor, on his way into the offices of his production company that morning, saw a silhouette which, from behind, reminded him of the model in the poster. He had never seen the model except in that photo, taken head-on, but he decided that, from behind, the resemblance was striking. The young woman who had just disappeared around the corner of the hallway was not very tall; she was wearing not a green suit, but a flowing black skirt and a badly cut jacket. Only her chestnut hair evoked the model's blond mane. Thus Mademoiselle Monnier entered the Counselor's employ. He liked to see her from behind; when he saw her face, he told himself that Mademoiselle Monnier's blue eyes looked like marbles that had rolled in sand a bit too often, that her nose lacked delicacy, that her lipstick was too dull. The Counselor promised himself he would adjust, paint, disguise reality. Mademoiselle Monnier played the sleeping beauty, the woman who languishes after a savior, a man with beautiful white hands who would know how to reinvent her. The Counselor, convinced he had a moron on his hands, felt himself overcome by a sense of mission: to dress the docile toy who sat humbly at her post in front of his office, to fix his seal on her, to imprint the brand name on her skin.

While I was in the Counselor's office one morning, Mademoiselle Monnier made her entrance. She was wearing a dark green suit. Her hair, dyed blond, had been cut short. She walked toward us and deposited a file in front of the Counselor with a scarlet-painted smile. From where I sat, I had Mademoiselle Monnier in the foreground and the photograph of the model in the background. The Counselor turned out to be a remarkable plagiarist. In the gaze he rested on Mademoiselle Monnier could be read the satisfaction of the Creator who, on the seventh day, considered his work and saw that it was good. His attitude expressed a happiness that was all the more vivid for having been won against all odds, as well as the regret of acknowledging that everything can be gotten on the cheap, even dreams. He felt a certain gratitude toward this young woman who played Mademoiselle Ersatz with such ingenuity, and a certain contempt for someone who would allow herself to be molded like that, a great pride at having succeeded in cosmetically enhancing reality, a certain bitterness at having obtained only a surrogate for his dreams, and a growing shame at having given himself over to a pathetic swapping game that made a mockery of his intelligence. That day, I, too, thought Mademoiselle Monnier was a moron, one of those women you expect to play the potted plant, women whose role consists in a single reply: Make me whatever you want me to be. ¶ Several months after the metamorphosis of Mademoiselle Monnier, I met her on the rue François-Ier on the arm of a heavyset young man. A lock of blond hair fell across his forehead, and his shirt was open to reveal a gold chain around his neck. Mademoiselle Monnier was dressed in green. She smiled at me without stopping. ¶ After that meeting, Mademoiselle Monnier would keep me with her every time I came out of the Counselor's office; she would offer me cups of coffee while outlining her concept of love to me, giving me recipes for how to get the best of it. A strategist was hiding behind that moronic smile. She let the Counselor play dolls with her as much as he liked. She was fully aware of the advantages she derived in exchange: she was learning how to dress, how to make herself up, how to stand, and how to speak. The Counselor would ask her to change her lipstick, to try a certain perfume, to buy a certain kind of shoes. He was happy just playing dolls; he had never once undressed her, had never once tousled her hair, had never even laid a hand on her. The Counselor did not take her home with him; he sometimes saw her home in the evening, but he left her at the door of the building. Mademoiselle Monnier wondered if the delicacy the Counselor displayed toward her wasn't proof of some hidden vice—but she didn't have a tormented nature and therefore neglected to interrogate herself on the reasons for his conduct. ¶ Green was Mademoiselle Monnier's lucky color. Since she had begun dressing in the Counselor's fetish color, men had been pursuing her avidly. Mademoiselle Monnier did not want to spoil the Counselor's work. So her company was available in exchange for money. Her reputation was growing among a small circle of initiates, but she was, she said, very exacting in the selection of her guests.

23

Her goal escapes me. What drives her to amass peculiarities, to warp her destiny, to strive for defects, only defects? She lives on rejection, feeds on betrayals. To the pride of being a *métèque,* a swarthy foreigner, writing in a language that is not her own, she wants to add the suspicion of illegitimacy, her semicertainty that she is of mixed blood. She wants to put the solidity of her nerves to the test. The example of my failure gives her the courage to go exploring the frontiers of mental health. The memory of my downfall fifteen years ago incites her to let herself sink in order better to spring back. I've prepared the way. I am her hellebore. Her miracle cure for madness. ¶ She has always given herself over to that game which consists in looking only at the shadow projected by things and never at the things themselves. If she keeps playing the game too long she'll endanger her nerves; lying in bed in the evening she'll rub her temples, feeling that her head is nothing but a ball of flesh bristling with nails. ¶ They got to me, but they won't get to her. Her reasoning is identical to mine: if it is illegitimacy then it won't be madness, with my help she will elude it. She defended herself against the threat of madness by becoming her own double. She wanted to make herself a stranger to the family, then to her country, then to her native language, and finally to herself. ¶ She tells me she is suffering from precocious disillusionment, that she feels an instinctive distrust of life, that for a long time her relations with the outer world have given her suffocating attacks of panic—for years she has lived like the ancestor, chained up at the back of a cage. She had to chain herself up in order to preserve herself. She was afraid of life because her mother represented life, life in its most loathsome form. Egotistical,

belligerent life, life in all its vulgarity, lewd life, vora-
cious life, animal life, life that is submissive when it finds
itself confronting a force greater than itself but crush-
ing when it runs up against something weaker. Life has
always repelled her—when she imagines herself living,
she imagines herself living like her mother. She chained
herself up, she placed herself under house arrest. She
believed she was in danger. On the one hand there was
life, which she always thought of as two steel jaws, two
open thighs, greedy for firm flesh. On the other hand
was madness. It was either loathsome, viscous life, or
another life, a free life, a life lived according to her own
desires and not according to norms—and in that case,
madness would stalk her. ¶ She had a choice between the
example of her mother and my own example. Either she
lived like an animal, like the queen of the insects, moving
forward, her poisoned antennae held out in front of her,
destroying all other lives in order to ensure her own. Or
she went beyond that and floundered into madness. She
defended herself, she chained herself up so as to follow
neither her mother's example nor mine. ¶ In this family,
putting your brain to work, cultivating your lucidity, is
a sign of dementia. In this family, you are advised not to
explore the folds of consciousness, not to shine too much
light into your head. In this family, the shadowy zones
are preferred. In this family, only gold glitters, all other
lights are dangerous, all other lights are to be forbidden.
My mistake was not to respect the half-light in which
everything is permitted—hate, lechery, low blows dealt
to those closest to you. ¶ Precocious disillusionment, *she*
says, is a dangerous illness, one that can turn out to be
fatal. The disease preserves the youth of those who suffer
from it, but attacks their vital functions. In appearance,
the sufferer is young, healthy, but his blood is poisoned,
his head is sick, his nerves are trammeled. ¶ Precocious
disillusionment has been her weapon of defense, the evil

she has used to defend herself against the evil represented by her mother's will to live. She has been like a starving woman who puts herself on a diet. ¶ Since her mother's revelation, she glimpses the possibility of loosening the stranglehold. As if she had lived all those years with a bird on her arm, a bird of prey that was digging its claws into her flesh—blood ran from her wound, and with each passing day the claws sank deeper until they merged with her veins. Her mother reveals a secret to her, and suddenly it's as if she no longer had to endure the weight of the bird of prey on her arm, as if she could finally chase it away, clean the wound. ¶ She knows that any manifestation of life has always been pitilessly stamped out. She abstained, out of fear of being pulverized. Her father was crushed. I was crushed. In one way or another, the family eliminated both of us. The family eliminated her father by constricting his vital space, keeping him from breathing, allowing him no function other than that of lackey, forbidding him to be anything but a perfect zero. The family eliminated me by isolating me. It hung a sign around my neck that said *Stark raving mad,* and it was as if I were dead. I *was* dead in a way, because they had destroyed the only link that made me a citizen of this life. ¶ In this family, they don't say I am crazy, they prefer to say, *He is sick. Crazy* is a word rarely spoken in this family, out of superstition. They know they are all lunatics, but as long as it can't be seen it must not be said. Madness stalks them. In my case, the sickness has declared itself. In their cases, it smolders, it leaves its ravages. It crumples up their souls, it bloodies their dreams, it forces them to take flight. What they call *madness* in me is nothing but my refusal to follow their straight and narrow way, to sit in my corner and keep myself calm in order to keep my genes from rising up within me. What they call my *sickness* is only a sudden change of character: one day I decided to obey my feelings and not follow the rules of conduct they dictated to me any longer. I behaved scandalously. All the more scandalously for having, according to them, revealed the family's hidden madness. I shattered the petty order that had been established. In their eyes, I fell sick. But simultaneously I fell into disgrace. In their eyes, I'm the one who wasn't able to manage his madness, control his savage instincts. They accused me of lechery, immorality. I was no longer the heir, the family's only son. They said they wanted to cure me. What they really wanted was to lock me up so I could no longer spoil the view, the little view they had of their narrow lives. They think they have triumphed over madness, but they've done no more than shrivel up, shrivel up until madness can no longer have a hold on them. ¶ They couldn't stand it that I sent their lovely plan packing, their rules to live by. They couldn't stand it that I went it alone. They have always thought they had to march with their ranks tightly closed to conceal the leering shadow that follows them; they have always thought that by making common cause, they would succeed in selling their shadow, their madness, back to the devil. They haven't forgiven me for letting go of them, for making myself inaccessible to their noxious protection. They have only one thought: to stay together, to be mad among themselves, and to make the world believe they are healthy and prosperous.

24

The Counselor says, I'm going to go off and get married
by the sea. In autumn. We'll take a room in one of the
hotels that is emptying out for the season. We'll ask the
porter and the chambermaid to be our witnesses.

(*In a low voice,* I'm trying to exhaust my energies with
crying jags. I empty myself out in order to sleep. Crying
jags are replacing sleeping pills.) Sunday mornings, the
Counselor's eyes are red, his eyelids are swollen, his face
is puffy. Sunday mornings, the Counselor goes to the buf
fet in the Gare du Nord, installs himself at a table, drinks
beer and doesn't move from his seat until evening.

The Counselor says, I will get married on a very windy
day. She will wear a green suit.

(*In a murmur,* Sunday was invented for our humiliation.
I should never stop. A toy clown moves forward because
someone has wound it up. When it stops moving, it feels
like laughing in its own face.) The Counselor's elbows
drag across the grimy table; he stares straight ahead and
notices, from time to time, the smell of fried food.

The Counselor says, After the ceremony, I'll go sit with
her on the terrace of the restaurant facing the beach.
Together we will look at the sea.

(*Carefully articulating his words,* Sundays, I observe the
protocol of disgust. I'm like a boneless bird. I'd like to be
locked up at the bottom of a cage, my head between my
knees, then taken somewhere else, thrown into the sea,

the way they used to get rid of bastard children, and left
to drift on the water.)

The Counselor says, She will wear a green suit. I will
place my hand on the back of her neck, between the tuft
at the base of her hairline and the collar of her jacket. We
will look in the same direction.

(*Wiping beer foam from the corner of his mouth,* When the
clown comes back from the seaside with the Love of His
Life, he will triumph over Sundays, but he will still go
forward without knowing very well why; he will no longer
dare spit, for fear that the spittle will fly right back in
his face.)

The Counselor says, In the train that will bring us back
from the sea, we will sit side by side, we will hold hands
without speaking.

(*With a snicker,* Man is indeed an animal that feeds on the
fictions it invents to safeguard itself. You hold a brain-
less nitwit in your arms and call her My Soul, you marry
a moron and call her Love of My Life. You fall asleep
in a foul-smelling bedroom—the promises you made to
yourself and broke stink like a sewer. You wake up in the
morning and find yourself clasped in the arms of your
own rancor. What you call meeting and coming together
is nothing more than an illicit arrangement: you give the
unsold inventory of your life and in return you receive
unpaid invoices. You dream of a happiness like a cloud
streaked with pink, and you embrace a pouch of vomit.)
That Sunday morning, before arriving at the Gare du
Nord, the Counselor called me from his car to ask me, in
a dry voice that left me no option of declining, to join him
at the grimy table in the station buffet.

*   *   *

III

The Counselor says, You will write an episode of *The Love of Their Life*. I will dictate it to you, if necessary. I will erase all those dark thoughts from your head, I will purify your brain. I will force-feed you with joy. I will teach you the mathematics of sentimentality, the hearts-and-flowers method. I will tear you away from Ricin's influence.

(*Almost without opening his lips,* The swindle must be perpetuated, a world must be created for teenage salesgirls, the requiem of lonely men must be sung and one must do one's part to make people believe that love saves the day.)

The Counselor says, You are under Ricin's control. He knocks on your door and you open it. He goes for nighttime walks and you walk beside him. He tells you about his contempt for women and you approve. He denigrates your loves and you tell him he's right. He sabotages your plans and you're grateful to him. He does his little number as the virtuoso of slander and you admire him. But look at him, he's nothing but a lame dog that's always pissing beside the fire hydrant. He creates a void around you so as to have full domination over you. He calls himself your brother. He behaves like your conscience's pimp. He dresses your mind. He kneads your ideas. He has you, he keeps your head under water. He keeps you from breathing anything but the smell of the morgue he drags around with him. Ricin's pockets are filled with ashes. He will force them down your throat, he'll fill your mouth with them so you will come to resemble him, a bitter fruit. Ricin's life is a botched pirouette.

(*Between his teeth,* Me, too. I'm in the process of botching my pirouette and finding myself flat on my ass.)

The Counselor says, When I have returned from the seaside, I will no longer come and sit at this grimy table on

Sundays. On Sundays, I will go out for walks with her, she will wear a green suit, we will make plans for our life together.

(*Holding back a belch,* The truth is that I aspire to a small life in a vacuum-sealed container.) The Counselor slides a hand under his jacket and scratches his belly with a grimace of disgust (Still, it's something to jerk off with clichés of mediocre happiness in your head), he loosens his tie, sticks a finger into the buttoned-up collar of his shirt and scratches the skin on his neck. The room's neon lights suddenly come on. The Counselor puts his hand in front of his eyes, turns his head aside, pulls his chair toward the dark corner of the wall (My soul is so damaged that the light of day hurts me), the beautiful white hand moves quickly, to the belly, the arms, the thigh, as if it were chasing an insect across the body (My body is burning, my body is red with confusion). Seated at the grimy table, in the dark corner of the room, the Counselor promenades his hand frenetically over his body, which is covered with stigmata (Sometimes I even get an itching on my feet, I have to get up and go to the men's room, take off my shoes and scratch the soles of my feet). The Counselor bursts out in a lugubrious laugh (I am a pustule with white hands, a diseased eruption, a *Vesuvius of pain.* Across my whole body, I feel the touch of a white-hot knife laid flat against my skin).

The Counselor says, Ricin wants you sick, he wants you dead. He dreams of seeing you hanging from the bars of his window, your face decomposed, body rotting. When I come back from the seaside, I will teach you the unknown principle of joy. And Ricin will no longer be able to bank on you as if you were a yearling colt he can deck out in his mourning colors.

*   *   *

(*With a sigh,* A long time ago, I read something that began, *And I will offer you women of luxury.* I was convinced that the phrase hadn't presented itself to me by chance, that the hypothesis was something to be taken seriously: life would offer me luxurious women, women of a necessary futility who would glide there, into the space contained between my two open hands. I had only to act as if I wanted to keep them and knead them between my fingers. *Letting out a belch,* I had been promised luxurious women. I stayed there, openmouthed, in expectation of their arrival. I waited. After a while, waiting made me into a little old man who is devoured by the little spiders of reality; they suck his blood, they nest under his arms, they guzzle his vital fluids. On Sundays, the little old man sits down at the table of the retirement home. He laps up his dishwater; from time to time, spoon in the air, he looks at the bottom of his bowl, his little moldy head dreams of fresh bread, succulent meat, the thighs of a luxurious woman, but a spider bite brings him back into order, so he dips his spoon into the bowl, he eats his dishwater, scratching his crotch.)

The Counselor says, I am going to go off and get married by the sea. Beforehand, I will have given the tableau its final touches. With her green suit, she will look like a luxurious woman. I will be enveloped in a long black coat. I will look like a monk. After the ceremony, we will go and sit on the terrace of the restaurant facing the beach, then we will take the train back . . .

(*In a stifled voice that seems to come from his belly,* . . . As we get off the train, I'll leave her standing there, there on the platform, I'll tell her, NEVER TRY TO SEE ME AGAIN, and I'll take the first exit.)

25

Tonight I'm waiting for a visit from the white butterfly.
I've put my room in order. Only a pencil and my gray
notebook, the letter in its envelope and a pair of scissors
are left on the table. I've put the books borrowed from
the library away in the wardrobe. On its door, Käthe K.
watches me with benevolence. She wants to play the
good mother, to know nothing of the baseness being prepared there under her eyes. I hate her pointed face. I hate
guardian angels. She won't have the satisfaction of seeing me collapse and beg her forgiveness. I pull the photo
down, rip it into pieces and throw it away. I sit down at
the table and open the notebook which I close immediately. I'm suffocating. I get up. I open the window. It's
cold outside. I lean out into the night. I turn my back
on the monster that is prowling around the room, its tail
held high. It awaits its prey, it pants lasciviously. It hopes
to get something for its money. Soon I'll hear the wings
of the white butterfly ripping under its bellowings. ¶ The
scissors that are on the table were deep in my pocket
yesterday. From my window, I had seen the man from the
third floor go out with a shopping bag. For the past several days, he had gone out himself to replenish his supply
of alcohol. Over his undershirt, he was wearing a short,
thick coat. I threw on my jacket and went down to the
lobby. I lurked around the elevator, waiting for him to return. My right hand, deep in the jacket pocket, squeezed
the pair of scissors. He came back before long. The bottles
were clinking in his bag. He pushed the button for the
elevator. I got in behind him. I saw the back of his thick
neck. My hand squeezed the scissors deep in my pocket.
I would only have had to make a single movement. He
turned around and offered me his drunken moon of a

face. His breathing was labored and he stank of sweat and vomit. My gaze focused on a point behind the right ear where the soft, fatty flesh was begging to be bled. One move and blood would spurt out onto the side of the elevator. It stopped at the third floor. I would only have had to make a single movement. I let go of the scissors. My hand reached into the pocket of my pants and brought out a bill that I handed to the man as he went through the door of the elevator. He took the bill. He said, Tomorrow night. The door closed on the smell of sweat and vomit. ¶ The scissors are on the table and the monster is snickering behind my back. Aren't you fine. Aren't you clean. No blood on your hands, your cock washed, your crotch scrubbed with soap. You're waiting for the reward for your cowardice. Your cock is swelling with impatience. It hasn't been used in years, it is very grateful to your head for its heroic impulse. You were right not to play savior. There's no place for purity in this room. The walls must be spattered with your delirium. Turn out the lamp. Shut the curtain. Darkness silences guilt. All you have to do is open the door. You're not her first torturer. Her wings are already ripped. She lives from her wound. She expects you to perpetuate the chain of baseness. ¶ I turn off the light and wait, seated at the table. It is midnight. Through the stairway, the purring of the elevator comes up. It stops on the fifth floor. I listen. Steps go off in the direction away from my room. My gaze turns from the door, the awful apple green door with its peephole that lets in the light from the hallway. The scissors are on the table. At my back, the monster snickers. It salivates, it sighs with pleasure. I am the executor of its base deeds. Soon I will open the door, I will let the white butterfly in and the trap will snap shut on her wings. ¶ Footsteps approach my room. Three furtive knocks on the door. I stay seated, tense, on my chair. The monster behind me grows agitated, it breathes heavily, its breathing quickens. The smell of sweet flesh makes its nostrils palpitate. I would like to stand up, open the latch, and leave the white butterfly to face the monster, but I don't move. The scissors are on the table. Again a knock, very light, like an animal brushing against the door. Behind me, the monster is breathing harder and harder, like a hunting dog running itself out of breath after the prey it sees disappearing into a thicket. Instead of standing up, I pick up the scissors from the table. In my fist, the glittering blade. I am immobile. From outside, a hand softly turns the doorknob. The monster screams. It commands me to get up. I hold up the scissors. I strike. The blade sticks out at the top of the thigh. I stifle a cry. Blood pours down my pants. I hear footsteps moving away down the hall and the elevator starting up. Then I don't hear anything. The scissors have fallen to the ground. I rest my head on the table, I turn my eyes toward the open window. I feel the fresh air on the back of my neck. The monster has vanished into the night.

26

Mademoiselle Monnier died wearing a green suit. On a very windy day. The bullet was shot into the back of her neck, between the tuft at the back of her artificially blonde hair and the collar of her jacket. Mademoiselle Monnier died on a Saturday in autumn, at coffee time, while sitting on the deserted terrace of a beachfront restaurant. The waiter had just set the cups of coffee on the table that the hotel's only two guests, arrived that very morning, had asked him to set up, despite the wind and the threat of rain, at the far end of the empty terrace. The man was enveloped in a long black coat with a turned-up collar that hid half his face; the woman was wearing a green suit. They had ordered two coffees. The waiter had set the two cups on the table, then went back inside the deserted restaurant to read the newspaper. A shot rang out. The waiter cocked his ear. There was music in the restaurant, seagulls crying on the terrace. Through the picture window, the waiter could see that the man in the black coat had risen and was standing behind the woman in the green suit. The waiter went back to his newspaper. Several minutes later, another shot rang out. The waiter turned up the radio. When he raised his head from the newspaper, he saw through the picture window that the woman in the green suit was still seated while behind her the man in the black coat lay flat on the planks. Mademoiselle Monnier died with her face turned toward the sea, a moronic smile frozen on her lips. ¶ The day before their departure, the Counselor bought himself the long black coat, though it was too warm for the season. He had told me to meet him at his office, and he arrived enveloped in his black garment. Mademoiselle Monnier made a brief appearance during the interview. The coat

lay on the armchair in a corner of the room. She wanted
to pick it up and put it on a hanger; it slipped from her
hands and fell on the carpet with a dull thud. The Counselor observed Mademoiselle Monnier's movements with
impatience. She remarked that the coat was very heavy,
As if you were carrying stones in your pockets. The Counselor said dryly, Leave it there! Mademoiselle Monnier
stood up immediately and left the room, abandoning
the coat on the floor, at the foot of the armchair. The
Counselor announced that his production company was
bankrupt. He would not sign the contract that had been
agreed upon. No doubt, this was of no importance to me
whatsoever since, he said, I had never had the slightest in-
tention of writing an episode of *The Love of Their Life*. The
Counselor spoke without looking at me, eyes fixed on his
hands which rested flat on the table, his beautiful white
hands which were trembling a little. You came here to be
a voyeur. I hope you will enjoy the show. ¶ The Counselor
asked me to come back and see him again the next day;
he wanted to leave me a souvenir, a gift he had intended
for Mademoiselle Monnier and which I could save as a
relic. The next day, when I arrived at the production company's offices, I found the door open, the offices silent. In
the Counselor's office, nothing had moved. There was one
sign of disorder: the shelves to the right of the door were
empty. On the floor was the debris of broken plaster,
marble, wood. The Counselor had meticulously destroyed
every object in his collection, had smashed the hands cast
in bronze with a hammer. On the wall, the model in the
green suit was smiling. On the almost empty table I found
a box. It contained a small hand made of black wood, on
its fourth finger was a ring set with a red stone. ¶ That
morning, the Counselor had left with Mademoiselle Monnier for the seaside. They had fled emptyhanded, he in
his black coat, she in her green suit. They took the train,
rented a room at the beachfront hotel. They were sitting

on the terrace of the restaurant, had ordered two coffees. The Counselor kept his hands in his coat pockets. The waiter left the cups on the table and went back inside. The Counselor stood up; he placed himself behind Mademoiselle Monnier. For the first time, they were looking in the same direction. Mademoiselle Monnier was smiling. The Counselor slipped his beautiful white hand into the inner pocket of his long coat. The shot rang out at coffee time, he said to himself. The detonation made him jump. Then the beautiful white hand aimed the gun at his stomach. The barrel sank into a mass of soft flesh. It made the Counselor think of a down pillow. He shut his eyes. It was too sweet.

27

Night is falling. The library closes in five minutes. I'm
lurking at the far end of the back room. On a cart nearby
is the pile of books I was supposed to shelve this afternoon. From the front, the voice of the librarian drifts
back to me. She is sending away the last readers. I hear
her straightening up the card catalogue, shutting drawers.
Then the front door opens and shuts in a clatter of locks
being bolted. A quarter of an hour before closing time,
I got up from the table where I had been sorting index
cards, dragging my right leg; I nodded to the librarian
who gazed at me compassionately and lowered her eyes
toward the bandage that was evident under my pants; she
advised me in her educated doll's screech to get some
rest, to sleep—she's worried because I don't look well.
I put my coat on, but leave the door ajar; I stand in the
hallway of the building, waiting, smoking a cigarette.
Through the half-open door, I see the librarian get up and
walk away from her table. I slip back inside, disappear
into the men's room; then, when she has gone back to
her place, I dash back to the far end of the library. I'm
locked in for the night. The librarian has always been
careful not to entrust me with the keys. When the cleaning lady comes tomorrow morning, I'll have to employ
another subterfuge, slip outside behind her back and
come back an hour later, after the librarian has arrived.
It's cold. The boiler is shut off at night. I'll bundle up
in my coat to sleep. ¶ From the library's windows I can
see the Pommeraie Hotel in the distance, the two red
buildings facing each other and the stretch of lawn between them. Tonight again the elevator will stop at the
fifth floor, a little white shadow will slip down the corridor, scratch at the door of number 505, wait in vain for a

response and leave noiselessly. Tomorrow morning, I'll go back to the Pommeraie, I'll hang around in the lobby, in front of the elevator, a bill rolled up inside my fist. I'll see the man from the third floor coming home with his shopping bag. He'll take the elevator, I'll follow him in and the bill will change hands.

So here you are, a savior. For how long? Two, three days maybe, until your hunger forces you to keep the bill for your daily meals? Two or three nights until the library walls are exuding temptation, until your body, bundled up in the coat, is trembling with desire and regret? Tonight you won't sleep, you'll go leafing through books searching for a recipe for ataraxia, but your eyes won't be able to focus on the words — your retina is haunted by the white silhouette that slips down the deserted hallway.

I go from one row of shelves to the next. The bandage around my thigh hampers my steps a little. My shoes squeak on the linoleum. I have the feeling that someone is there, behind me, following me, glued to my heels. *You paid so she could sleep in her bed like a nice little girl.* I stop from time to time in front of a row of shelves, a book I don't think I've paged through yet, whose title I try to decipher on the old binding. I haven't turned on the lights. *You paid to satisfy your Samaritan perversity.* The room is illuminated only by the streetlights outside. In the back corner, near the cart, the gray notebook, the sketchbook, some pencils, a pocket flashlight and some batteries are hidden in a sack. *She's your little victim, she belongs to you, you don't touch her, you play at saving her.* ¶ I need a book. I know exactly the sentence I need at this moment (We are thick-skinned animals, we hold out our hands to each other, but it's useless, we only scrape our rough leathers against each other — we are very much alone). *You're lying to yourself. Turn some pages.* (I will tear her coat from her shoulders and throw her down, naked, her carcass in the sunlight.) *That's what you have in mind. Her skin is dark, sweet, under the white hooded coat. You would like to take the coat off, trail your tongue across her belly, bite her until she bleeds, leave the marks of your teeth on her little breasts, grab her hair in your fists, hurt her, lick the tears that fall onto her cheeks, then throw her out, send her back to the life she has known until now.* ¶ Her rotting carcass, naked, in the sunlight. And me, enveloped in my coat, pressed against the books in the back corner. I don't want to save her. I'm putting my powers of resistance to the test. I'm paying to torture myself, to add further privations to my solitude. I want to be hungry and not eat. I want to be nice and warm and yet allow myself to be locked up in this room with its gusts of icy air. I want the little girl in the white hooded coat, and at the same time as I save her from others I am saving her from myself.

It's that letter with the pretentious handwriting that put an end to my peace of mind. She sent me back to the family, to sickness. She forced me to look at myself in the mirror—all the gesticulations I made in my attempt to be a man in the crowd, a gray man indistinguishable from other men, were for nothing. Madness is in me, my face is frozen into an insane grimace. The letter with the pretentious handwriting arrived to mock my ambition to be a placid man. The woman who wrote that letter didn't know what she was doing. She demands that I assume my role as madman. She preaches the pride of differ-ence. What does she know about quarantined humanity, shadows with broken voices, little animals whose skins have been burned by unhappiness, fugitives who scat-ter in all directions without finding an emergency exit? ¶ My eyes wander from one row of shelves to the next, but the miracle does not take place. Since the letter arrived, books have been silent. In one blow, my calm has departed and in its place I find a vacant lot, and I see myself there in the middle of it: I am a dog, an old, tired dog. I bark, I want someone to open the door for me, but there are no houses anywhere nearby. In the emptiness that has set in, I try to hang on to books; they saved me once, they'll save me again. Since the letter arrived, books have no longer come alive in my hands. I've lost the thread. My companions have turned their backs on me. I'm not talking about little potbellied dandies who release their little works the way a cow releases its turds or about geese who preen their quills in front of a mirror. I'm talking about masters who helped me believe I was an ascetic, my passions extinct, a solitary booklover. All these years, I've lived with books, through books. They formed a rampart around me. The letter arrived, the rampart fell down and again the winds of madness blow. I'm alone in the middle of a vacant lot. I bark. Never again will any door open to my appeal. I hide my eyes behind my paws. Howls rasp through my throat. ¶ My solitude was no more than the mark of my madness. I'm not inaccessible, I've been liquidated. I didn't choose to hold back, I was given up for dead. The letter destroyed my illusions. I was living my solitude like a victory, when in fact I've done nothing but exchange one cell for another, leaving the company of sterile madmen for that of the wise—an asylum or a library, either way I'm still skimming off the droolings of other people's deliria. I am their brother with the hairy jowls. My head is burning but my blood is cold. ¶ The problem is how to avoid coming down with the fever, how to stay dry. Since the letter arrived, everything is dripping. I smell of damp sugar. I probe myself, touching all my sore spots. The Monk told me, If you want to approach the truth, keep silent. Don't mourn for yourself, or glorify yourself either. Don't deceive anyone, not even yourself. Don't start cherishing your defects, loving your own lame silhouette, don't be like the leper who sells his wounds. I was heading in the right direction. Everything started to go wrong after the letter arrived. Instead of approaching truth, I am going off to give my version of the lie. I'd like to strike right at the heart of the target, compose a report that will burn off all masks with its acid. I do nothing but tinkle my little chimes, ring the bells of distress. I sound the assembly of the phantoms, I open tombs, unearth corpses. But the cultivation of falsehood still flourishes, even six feet under. There I am, circling among the stacks like a crazy dog waiting to be put down. I'd like to lie down on the floor, feel the barrel of a gun between my two eyes, wait for the detonation that will heal me from this sentimental migraine. Everything is dripping. I'm dabbling at growing falsehoods, raising the leeches of nostalgia. When I dream of the white butterfly and the night that, thanks to me, she will spend in her bed like a nice little girl, I feel a need for fresh air in my chest. The thought of having saved her is enough to make my cock stand straight up. Though for many years the thing that hangs between my legs was satisfied with the automatic caress of my hand (I emptied myself without thinking of anything, especially not of ghosts), now, before giving any sign of life, it demands some sentiment, some sacrifice.

28

Ricin has made a foray into the shoe repairman's shop.
Early in the morning. The light hadn't been turned on
yet. At first he couldn't see anyone. He walked to the
counter, brushed his fingers over the shoetrees lined
up there in a long row. He was startled by a moan. He
pulled back his hand, turned. Behind him, in the dark
recesses of the shop, the mother was sitting in an armchair. An expression of intense pain twisted her mouth.
She closed her eyes as if she had been offended, as if Ricin
had surprised her when she was naked. The shoe repairman appeared in the doorway. He had a blanket under
his arm. His dog was behind him. The shoe repairman
leaped forward and stood so as to screen the old lady
from the visitor. The dog lay down near the mother's
chair. Ricin noticed a strange emptiness. As much as he
squinted, he couldn't make out the old lady's legs behind the shoe repairman's. The shoe repairman asked him
what he needed. At random, Ricin pointed to a pair of
wooden shoetrees. The shoe repairman didn't budge; he
looked at Ricin with hatred, his jaws clenched shut, and
told him to take the merchandise and leave the money on
the counter. The old lady behind him was making whim-
pering noises. Ricin took the pair of shoetrees. Before
leaving, he turned around. He saw the old lady pulling
on the back of her son's jacket. He saw the shoe repairman bend down to his mother and unfold the blanket to
put it over the emptiness that was where her legs should
be. The mother is nothing but a trunk sitting on that
armchair, Ricin says, The shoe repairman has nothing
but his dog and his half a mother. All he wants is to re-
place them with you. He wants a whole woman, a woman
who has legs and can follow him everywhere like a dog.

¶ That evening when I go out I don't see a trace of the
man with the dog in my street. He closed his shop earlier
than usual. Ricin says, I've scared the shoe repairman.
Now it's my turn to harass him. ¶ The days go by, the
man with the dog no longer stands guard in front of the
building. Ricin bought a pair of women's black pumps,
he leaves one of them at my house and breaks the heel of
the other which he keeps with him always, bulging in the
pocket of his coat. While waiting to push open the door
of the shoe repair shop again, he prowls. He never leaves
my neighborhood; early in the morning he sits in the café
that faces the shop, in a place where he can watch without
attracting any attention, and he observes the deeds and
movements of the man with the dog and his half a mother.
The old lady doesn't have a wheelchair. The shoe repairman carries her in his arms. In the morning, he parks his
car in front of the shop, opens the shutters and, before
even turning on the light, goes back to the car, takes his
mother in his arms, and carries her inside. He never fails
to glance up and down the street to make sure no one is
around. The old lady hides her head in the hollow of her
son's shoulder, she is afraid of the gaze of passersby. He
puts her down in the armchair and goes back to the car to
get the plaid blanket. The day Ricin went into the shop,
the shoe repairman had gone to walk his dog in the street
in front of my building, forgetting to spread the blanket
out over the armchair first. All day, the half a mother sits
enthroned in the corner of the shop. The dog lies nearby,
the son works behind the counter. It's a simple, peaceful
tableau, says Ricin. From time to time, at a sign from the
torso queen, the shoe repairman gets up from his chair
and carries her into the shop's back room. At noon, he
sets up a little table on some trestles and lays out dishes
that he prepared himself and brought with them that
morning. Sometimes, Ricin sees the old lady shaking her
head, refusing to eat, and the son feeding her himself

with a spoon. The old lady only eats one thing with relish: the little treat her son gives her every morning. He puts his mother down in the armchair and before walking his dog, buys something sweet for her at the corner. The old lady waits for him to come back, impatient. She rips the paper and pounces avidly on its contents. The shoe repairman goes out to walk his dog. Ricin says, The shoe repairman gives his mother a piece of sugar to gnaw and then, his conscience clear, he goes off to pace up and down in front of the door of your building. I see him hurrying off toward your street, and I see her devouring her sweet roll. She eats it with relish, picks up the crumbs that fall onto the blanket, licks her chops. It's the only moment of the day when, through the shop window, her face expresses a certain contentment. As soon as her son reenters the shop, she puts her torso queen face back on. She sits up straight in her armchair. She closes her eyes with confidence. Her son is there; he is watching over her. Ricin has been observing the shoe repairman and his mother for several days now; he is waiting for an event. He is waiting for something to go wrong. This morning, something went wrong. The old lady dozed off a moment in her armchair, her head thrown back. Then she reopened her eyes, with confidence, as usual. She reopened them, but this time she saw that the shoe repairman was not watching over her, that he was not bent over his work table, he was looking out toward the street. She knows that, except to greet a client or to look at her in order to anticipate all of her desires, her son never lifts his eyes from his work, her son never looks at passersby. She shuts her eyes with confidence, she opens them again and she surprises her son in the act of deceiving her. She turns her head toward the street, she sees you leaving the bakery, the same bakery, says Ricin, where the shoe repairman buys her treat for her. She sees you passing in front of the shop, your hair windblown and your legs agile. Her

128

son stopped working to watch you go by. The rest of the morning, she keeps her eyes riveted to the shoe repairman, to force him to lower his head toward the shoes. At noon, as on all the other days, the shoe repairman sets up the little table and sits down opposite her. Ricin says, I see the old lady pouncing on the food, eating greedily. The meal ended, the shoe repairman clears the table away and gets ready to go out with his dog. His mother calls him back. He runs to the rear of the shop and comes back with a basin. The old lady leans over and vomits up her meal. She has understood. She has understood why her son is always in such a hurry lately to leave her in the morning, at noon, in the evening, to go for a walk with his dog. She has understood why he buys the little treat for her in the morning. She has understood that she is no longer the queen. He doesn't carry her as if she were a baby anymore, he carries her as if she were a burden; he doesn't set her down gently anymore, he sets her down with relief. He doesn't carry her at all anymore, he endures her; he doesn't set her down in her armchair, he gets rid of her.

29

If I want my peace of mind back, I'll have to chase the author of the letter penned in midnight blue ink out of my head, throw away the gray notebook, send off a reply. *She* asks me to remember, to prove to her that the passing stranger's love for her mother was authentic (that's the word she uses), and meant to last (again, her expression). I'm going to inform her that this father in whom she places all her hopes loved with a futile love. I'm going to inform her that the *man of taste* only gave his love during the afternoon. ¶ On the table of the requisitioned hotel room there was champagne and grapes, near the window was a record player and some records of the latest hit songs, at the foot of the bed was a pair of red mules. When he found himself alone in this hotel room, the man of taste put the mules away in the closet and the hit songs in their jackets, opened the windows to dispel the smell of woman and sat down in an armchair to read while listening to a Chopin sonata. The man of taste went everywhere with his recordings of Chopin and Schubert, but the thought of introducing these companions of his solitude to his love never entered his mind. When he left the Country, the man of taste took the Chopin and Schubert records with him. To his love, he left the record player, the hit songs, and the pair of red mules. The record player found its place in the conjugal home, near the bedroom window. Over the years it wore out, crackling out tunes that had once been popular like an old lover with bad lungs who wants to acquit himself honorably nevertheless. ¶ The man of taste disappeared, his love went home, placed the record player near the window of the conjugal bedroom, the red mules at the foot of the bed. She lay down. For days, whole months, she lay in bed, she looked at the red mules at the foot of the bed. Her belly grew round, her mind came unhinged. She hummed the old melodies in order to remember, but what could she remember: her feelings had been requisitioned, her life had been occupied. And suddenly the ground was abandoned and only the hit songs were left to her, the silly anthems of a state of siege that had lasted one year. ¶ During the months following the departure of the man of taste, the record player played from morning to night in the conjugal home. It crackled out hit tunes, *My heart belongs to daddy . . .* The wife stayed in bed. *He's gone! He's gone!* The husband was there, ready to exhibit his status as the official cuckold and fill out the papers as the unofficial father. The wife stayed in bed. Her belly grew heavier. She sustained herself on sweets. *My vanished lover!* Her husband came and went in that house filled with hit songs that gave it a fraudulently festive atmosphere. ¶ *She* wrote me to find out which one her heart should belong to. The man of taste or the eternal husband? Throughout her childhood, her mother drummed those hit tunes into her. She would sing, *My heart belongs to daddy.* Regarding the eternal husband, it had often been repeated to her, *Your daddy is a nobody.* A nonentity. A man who wasn't even worth mentioning. Now, she hears her mother saying to her, *Nobody is your daddy.* You are the daughter of no one, the forgotten offspring of a runaway lover.

She is still at the stage of wondering if her mother and the man of taste copulated with feeling or if it was only a savagery which was dormant during the conjugal years that drove them into each other's arms. She has the vanity of the fetus who wants to sport the medal of love. She's still wondering if those two, the lovers in the requisitioned hotel room, were moved by a *sincere passion* (she has the naivete to believe that passion can be sincere: passion lies, but it lies in such a blinding flash that it is taken for

131

the truth). She is still wondering if her mother—when she left the house in the morning shortly after the eternal husband had done so, opened the door of the black Studebaker, settled behind the steering wheel and drove toward the city's grand hotel—went there out of love for the foreigner who had appeared in her life or out of boredom and in the hope of being able one day to liquidate the nonentity who served as her sparring partner, put the man of taste in a cage and make him repeat in his turn the role of the eternal husband.

She would like to write the romance of the black Studebaker, tell herself the story of a woman who perfumed her white gloves and slipped them on, despite the heat, before placing her hands on the steering wheel, paint a portrait of a man of taste who may have read ancient Japanese poetry, who may have said to his love,

Don't be deceived
you don't know who I am
but night after night
the one you see in your dream
I am that one.

She'll have to make do with the chronicle of a wartime adultery; she'll have to remember that the man of taste went to his amorous rendezvous accompanied by armed soldiers, and that shortly after the man of taste said his farewells to the Country, the black Studebaker, mothballed in front of the conjugal home, was found one morning riddled with bullet holes.

She would like to believe in her mother's passion, in the passion of a woman whose emotional energy was not sufficiently challenged by marriage for a visitor who had come only in the hope of reawakening an appetite for life. If she yields to the temptation to call herself the child of that

love, she'll be nothing but the child of the requisitioned
hotel room, the child of champagne and hit songs, the
child of the bubblehead and the sniper who had some
good times together on the killing fields.

Since she can't tell herself the story of a *sincere passion,*
she'd like to make do with the image of a gloved woman
behind the wheel of a black Studebaker, the image of
the heroine of a television series driving to the rhythm
of hit songs toward a love that wasn't supposed to have
any consequences. She would like to hold herself to that
image, to efface the epilogue, not to know that shortly
after the departure of the man of taste, the men in black
launched an offensive against the city, that they machine-
gunned the Studebaker parked in front of the conjugal
home. By then, the T.V. movie heroine had taken off her
white gloves. The record player crackled out hit songs,
Are you lonesome tonight? She stayed in bed, her belly
heavy, her gaze turned toward the front of the house
where the Studebaker riddled with bullet holes still remained. Several years later, the men in black took power.
They had finally driven away the man of taste and his suc-
cessors. The Studebaker had been sent to the junkyard.
The records of the hit songs were thrown onto the fire.
Shall I come back again . . . ? The heroine no longer wore
her white gloves. With the eternal husband, she went to
watch the foreign army's soldiers and officers who were
fleeing in helicopters. Women grabbed the doors of the
helicopters, waiting for the love of their life to take them
away with him, but the love of their life hit their grace-
ful little fingers with the butt of a rifle to make them let
go. The women collapsed on the ground, but still they
stretched out their arms toward the love of their life,
they stretched out their arms because they were afraid,
afraid of the men in black who were coming out of the forests and taking power in the cities, afraid of the men with

their stern voices and severe demeanor who, they were convinced, were going to avenge themselves on them, on the women, for the years when the women let themselves float along on the sweetness of living with the love of their life. The women stretched out their arms less from regret than from fear. They stretched out their arms, but the love of their life had only one pressing thought: to get out of this *shithole* as quickly as possible. ¶ Shortly after his departure, the man of taste sent a pink layette and a blanket to the Country; the next year it was a tea set, after that some expensive fabrics, and always records of hit songs. Does *she* remember those gifts which, her mother said, came from a man of taste, a *gentleman*? *She* didn't know then that the gentleman's given name was, except for two letters, very much like the international first name that had been chosen for her. The gentleman's presents arrived in the Country and were delivered to the conjugal domicile. She saw her mother feverishly tearing open the packages. The morning after those gala days, her mother would put a new record on the record player, *I want to be loved by you, just you!* and go to bed. For weeks she stayed in bed. Life in the conjugal domicile ground to a halt. The tea cups were too fragile, the blanket too warm and the fabrics too precious to be used. The Studebaker riddled with bullet holes stayed in front of the house. The child with the international given name went to school on foot. Despite the heat, she wore a white blouse buttoned up to the collar, white bobby socks and little white gloves that made her palms itch. She was inseparable from the eternal husband, the man who had given her his name, *I want to be loved by you, just you!* and who answered the joyous melodies that the record player crackled out with an unsociable silence, *Nobody else but you.* ¶ For seven years following the departure of the man of taste the gifts arrived at regular intervals. The conjugal home was transformed into a shrine to The Great

Love. The woman stayed in bed, and all around her were arrayed the tea service and the records of hit songs, the silk dresses and the red mules, the record player and the precious fabrics, the thick envelopes containing wads of bills and the very thin envelopes containing letters that were shorter and shorter. The eighth year, the mailings suddenly stopped. The last gift was a pedal car, a miniature replica of the black Studebaker, except that the small model was painted blood red. When she came home from school, the child with the international first name settled in the white leather seat, placed her small gloved hands on the wheel, and rode the little car in circles in the front yard of the house beside the bullet-riddled Studebaker. ¶ She didn't like the blood-red pedal car. She didn't particularly enjoy toys, small replicas. She preferred the damaged model. She preferred to slide onto the front seat of the Studebaker. Around that time, the eternal husband would often take her to see gangster movies. She had kept some images in her head: the image of a car machine-gunned by some masked men, and of a dead gangster gunned down behind the wheel of his convertible riddled with bullet holes. As they left one of those films, the eternal husband bought her a pair of dark glasses, little hoodlum glasses. She wore pleated skirts and white blouses and ankle socks, but behind her mother's back she pulled her long hair back from her face, put on the hoodlum glasses, slid onto the front seat of the Studebaker, placed her little gloved hands on the wheel and imitated the gangster's death. She jerked as if she had been mowed down by a burst of machine gun fire. Then she played dead, her head thrown back. ¶ Until the day when she came home from school and found the front yard empty. There was a small oil stain on the gravel. The Studebaker had been taken away from its place in front of the house and sold to a junkyard. Inside, in the bedroom, the record player was spinning, *Shall I come back again?* For weeks, ever since the packages had stopped coming, she had walked straight past that bedroom. Her mother stayed in bed, face turned toward the wall. She went by on tiptoe, holding her breath so as not to breathe in the poisonous smell of the shrine to The Great Love, a smell of sweat and bad breath, urine and menstrual blood. That day, she stopped at the door of the bedroom filled with the suffocating smell and complete disorder. The shrine to The Great Love had been laid to waste. The silk dresses and the precious fabrics were in shreds, the tea service was a heap of shards, only the records of the hit songs seemed to be intact. Her mother was wearing the yellow satin ensemble that had a grimy collar and smelled of sweat. She was sitting on the floor, her back to the door. There was a chamber pot beside her and some matches. She was emptying out a cardboard box full of letters that she tore up and threw into the chamber pot. There was only one photograph left in the box, she struck a match, held the photo to the flame, and threw it, half aflame, into the chamber pot. The child walked past the room noiselessly. Behind the house, the pedal car was waiting for her. The white leather seats had been lacerated with scissors.

The man of taste knew how to shower women with red mules and silk dresses, jewels and enormous bouquets, he knew how to distract them with champagne and hit songs. Meanwhile, the man with the meager salary had nothing to offer. As a husband, he had never known how to make use of frivolities. As a father he was a taciturn presence. He liked churches and dark theaters. Does *she*, the author of the letter with the distinguished handwriting, remember that? ¶ I see them again, *her* and her father, one weekend afternoon at the movies. The theater smelled of piss, the wooden seats were uncomfortable, the film was a bad print of a crude comedy, but sitting there in the dark, he forgot that he was the man with the meager salary, the man who had missed his vocation and who could boast of only one thing: the name he had loaned the little girl so she could couple it with her international given name. *She* went with him to the dark theaters. It was their illicit recreation. Documentaries were shown before the film. One of them warned against child snatchers. It showed children abducted in marketplaces, in movie theaters. A man whose face could not be seen was the ringleader; he stole children and taught them to beg, to steal, and to abduct other children in their turn. There was a whole army of little wandering souls, each one designated by a number or an animal's name. At the time, *she* harbored no suspicions about her origins. Sitting there in front of the screen, she told herself that she had a family name and a given name, that she wasn't a stolen child, that she wasn't designated by a number, that she wasn't a little bird fallen out of the nest.

I see them again, *her* and her father, going to church very early in the morning when they wouldn't run into anyone else. I see them again lighting a candle without sending up any prayer. Now that she has grown up, now that she has left her father and the Country, she goes to museums. She remembers that the man with the meager salary went to churches and lit a candle in memory of the painter he had never known how to be. She remembers that the man with the meager salary was a deserter from his vocation, that he hung himself from a butcher's hook and let dogs rip out the best parts of himself. She wanders through museums and standing in front of achieved works of art she ponders her father's failure. When she hears her own steps resounding in the deserted rooms of museums she remembers the mornings when she went to church with her father. Their steps rang out on the flagstones.

*   *   *

That father's life was a ruin. Under the rubble lay the person he would have wanted to be, under the rubble lay a painter who did not know how to bring himself into being. Her life, too, is nothing but a ruin. Her fathers have sapped its foundations. She stirs the rubble, she clears away the debris, she can only put her hand on phantom fathers. She is a mole, burrowing, burrowing, to the melody of nostalgia.

The danger that lies in wait for her is a lyrical intoxication, a sentimentality that will corrode her cynical faculties. Her questions are laughable. Instead of asking herself who gave her life, she should tell herself that the person who allowed her to open her eyes to the world did nothing but allow her to see death. She should stick with this idea: those fathers didn't give her life, they gave her a thrashing. They demolished her. The first by bestowing an international given name upon her, the second by joining his name to it. In collusion with each other, her fathers gave her this small touch of originality and at the same time gave her the urge to flail about in an effort to live up to this little originality, this family name and given name joined together. Her fathers were her demolishers. They demolished her, but only by *giving* her the desire to live. They *gave* her that desire only to demolish her all the better.

30

The old lady is dead, said Ricin. The shoe repairman
laid her out on the bench behind the counter. The little
bench where normally the shoes needing to be resoled
are placed. He pushed all the shoes off and laid his half
a mother out on the bench, the blanket pulled up to her
chin. They arrived in the morning, the shoe repairman
gave her her treat, then went out to walk his dog. When
he came back he found her dead, her head fallen onto her
chest. ¶ Ricin entered the shop, the shoe with the broken
heel in the pocket of his coat. He saw the shoe repairman sitting there in the armchair, his arms dangling, and
the old lady lying on the bench. *She loved almond croissants,* said the shoe repairman, not looking at Ricin, his
eyes staring at the floor. *Every day I bought her an almond
croissant.* Then the shoe repairman was silent. He didn't
move from the armchair. The light, Ricin said, had not
been turned on. The old woman was lying on the bench,
beside her was the black dog, sniffing the shoes that lay
on the ground. The shoe repairman was sitting in the
armchair and I was standing, my hand in my coat pocket
caressing the shoe with the broken heel. I had no business
being there, in that shop, between your shoe repairman
and his half a mother, but I stayed there. A smell kept
me there. Then the shoe repairman said something like,
*That should have been enough for her. But no, she asked for
two almond croissants. She started eating for two.* I looked
at the old woman, said Ricin; one side of her face looked
happy while the other was frozen in an expression of pain.
I thought, A pregnant woman who died in childbirth. The
shoe repairman added something like, *She had become
strange, she was always afraid of catching cold, she had
sudden cravings or she would suddenly feel nauseated.* Ricin

said, The shoe repairman was talking in a muffled voice. I couldn't catch everything. On the counter lay the piece of paper that had been used to wrap up the two almond croissants. The shoe repairman muttered, *She was sure it was going to grow back.* Beside the paper was a small black bottle, upside down. And a smell that floated through the shop, a subtle smell, distinct from the smell of glue, old leather, and dog. The shoe repairman then said something like, *It couldn't go on any longer, she was repulsive.* Did he really say *repulsive*? The piece of paper was still on the counter. So the shoe repairman had undone the packet before giving the croissants to the old lady, the repulsive old lady. But what was in the little black bottle? The shoe repairman repeated, *Two almond croissants is too much.* Ricin said, He had forgotten I was there. He was sitting in the dead woman's armchair, his arms dangling, his head leaning to one side. On the chair lay a bit of croissant. The old lady must have dropped it. She died eating. She hadn't finished nibbling down her treat. *Repulsive,* said the shoe repairman, and he added, in his muffled voice, something like, *She once dreamed her legs were growing back. Afterwards, she waited. She waited for them to grow back. She even felt a tingling at the tips of her stumps.* The shoe repairman had placed his hands on his knees, which he rubbed and massaged as if to make a pain go away. He repeated, *She was repulsive, she sat there listening to her legs growing back. She sat there waiting for the first symptoms. She asked for two almond croissants. She was eating for two.* The dog got up, stuck its nose next to the old lady's face and began to lick her cheek. The shoe repairman didn't notice. Still rubbing his knees, he repeated the same sentence, *She was repulsive.* Ricin says, I got out of there, but the smell in that shop keeps coming back to me. It's a strange smell, a pleasant but horrifying smell. A smell of orange blossoms. A smell that makes me think of an orchard in the sunlight; suddenly the sky darkens and the orchard is invaded by a cloud of insects.

I listen to Ricin without a word. I think I recognize the smell, but I don't want to talk to him about it. It's the smell of a poison. A poison found in the body of an insect that lives in the desert. A poison that has a pleasant orange blossom scent and causes death almost instantaneously. A long time ago I read the story of an old blind man and his little granddaughter who lived in an abandoned train car on a battlefield. The old blind man was a former mercenary; from one of his expeditions he had brought back a capsule of poison, a poison that smelled like orange blossoms. He kept the poison in a suitcase that contained his uniform, a knife, some rusty bullets, and some photographs. He kept the capsule in a little pocket of the suitcase, promising himself that he would swallow it if it were ever his fate to be alone in the world. One evening, while the old blind man was dozing, his granddaughter opened the suitcase, discovered the capsule and swallowed the liquid, which smelled good, which smelled like orange blossoms. She died, curled in a corner of the car. The old blind man woke up, he called, no one answered. He waited a night and a day without leaving his bed. The following night, he told himself that he had been abandoned, that it was time for him to die. He got up and groped for the suitcase that contained the poison that smelled like orange blossoms.

31

I'm standing in the middle of this darkened room whose every corner I know. In front of me are the long shelves full of books. I hear them whispering. Their murmuring doesn't reach me. They've abandoned me. They've dismissed me from their fraternal union. They close themselves up at my approach like a chorus that turns its back on me and leaves me absolutely forsaken. Books can no longer do anything for me. What they think, I have pondered. What they contain, I have absorbed. Millions of words are crawling in my head, in my belly. But what I feel remains confused nevertheless. I can't keep playing hide-and-seek with the librarian, spending every night locked in here, rolled up in my coat, scribbling in this gray notebook that should be the answer to the letter with the distinguished handwriting but is no more than the water hole where I come to refresh my tired head. Behind me, through the window, lights in the distance mark the two buildings of the Pommeraie. I can't go back there, I can't take my place in the room with the apple green door and get up at night to watch the white butterfly crossing the lawn. I try to depict the features of the face hidden by the hood to myself, but I don't succeed. The white butterfly has no face; under the hood, it looks like a statuette carved out of brown wood. All the downtrodden are made of wood. It crosses the stretch of lawn with a light step. *Sadness is the taste of things*, when I think of the white butterfly this is the phrase that comes to my mind, this phrase copied out in my gray notebook on the first page. I have the taste of sadness on my tongue. Like a lozenge of ink that spreads its bile—a black liquid burns my palate, glides between my teeth, goes down into my viscera. It's been a long time since I felt that taste in my mouth, the taste of a poison that revivifies my blood and reheats my entrails. I find myself transported back years to the time when, in the Country, I would go to the madhouse, my little suitcase in hand. Tossed down next to the cart at the back of the library, the knapsack has replaced the little suitcase. I am there, reeling among the stacks, breathing in the vapor given off by all the cracked heads. Amid the smoke, I see a long body hung from the bars of a window, I see a white butterfly whose wings are stuck in the crack of an apple green door, I see two little gloved hands that are holding a letter. I would like to touch the hung body, I would like to grasp the wings of the white butterfly between my fingers, but the little hands holding the letter screen them out.

I slipped the letter and my notebook with its soft, gray cover into the knapsack. My writing hurts the eyes; it is miniscule, it scratches the paper as if I had used a hard, dry thorn instead of a pen. I reread the letter. I open my notebook. The letter and the report are written in French. *She* no longer knows her native language. For fifteen years I haven't spoken that language. There is no mention of the Country in the letter. There are only a few allusions to it in my report. We are from Nowhere, *she* and I. I won't go back to the Country; I will be the madman without a country. Back there lies the country of the hanged woman. The hanged woman's tomb is there. And mine. Here, my body has abandoned itself, and my head grows memories like poisonous flowers. If *she* has any sense, she'll understand that there is no going back for her. We are from Nowhere, she and I. She has to get that into her head. She must stop believing that some day she will find a family, a country. The Country has nothing to give her; since the men in black threw out the Foreigner, they are the Country's new fathers, and those new fathers have no use for her with her international first name. Those new fathers have no use for someone like me, someone who created a refuge for himself in madness. We are, *she* and I, wandering souls. Our roots go no deeper than the water's surface. She is looking for a father. I have my arms around the ghost of the hanged woman. We drift, hoping that the waters will take us toward the origin, but instead we are floundering in the dead arm of a river, we are continually working over the same obsessions, we are always carting around the same corpses.

This is the sixth night I've spent in the library. Rolled up in my coat, my belly empty, I squint and stare up at the darkness. Every night, just as I'm beginning to sink into sleep, a scream wakes me with a start. Two bums have stationed themselves in front of the metal shutter that covers the side entrance of the supermarket opposite the library. The first, young, robust, has the puffy face of a Christ who is choking back his tears. He spends the day sitting crosslegged on the ground, a blanket on his knees and another thrown around his shoulders. The second is a dapper little old man who wears a pale green checked shirt and a dark tie under a long navy blue coat. He spreads newspapers on the sidewalk before putting down his knapsack, his little things. Every morning he changes the cardboard he sits on, and every evening he shakes out the blankets before laying them down and wrapping himself up in them. During the day, he paces up and down without ever going far from his companion who doesn't move—even his face is motionless—a bottle of cheap wine within reach of his hand. As he walks, the old man gives little hops. Every three or four steps he stops with one foot in the air. In that position, he rummages through the nearby garbage can or stretches out his hand to passersby. They go to sleep very early, lying on top of the air vent. In the middle of the night, the young man lets out a scream. It's a sinister appeal, a cry that comes from very far away, from the *last station before Hell*. He screams like a sleeping man with a knife to his throat who lets out his death rattle just before his throat is cut. He screams like a dying man making a final effort to come back to life. Suddenly he stops struggling. The street falls silent once more. And fear rushes over me, my teeth chatter, I'm back in the asylum, my roommates are screaming, the Monk is dead, there is no one to save me now.

Six nights of reprieve. I think again of the only time I've gone into a movie theater — it was only a small theater with thick black curtains on the floor above the library. There was a screen and some plastic chairs. The place was almost empty. I sat down at the end of a row, near the door. The face of a hunted man loomed across the screen. He was entitled to six hours of reprieve. All night he wanders through the city; he knocks on doors, none of them opens. In the morning, he is caught. I remember the light trained on his face as he staggered back against the bars of a building. The film was called *Odd Man Out* or *Eliminé*. The bums made me think of the film again. I reel among the stacks. I'm in an arena. I walk out into the open. I'm looking for shelter. The books shut themselves at my approach. It's no use letting out screams in my gray notebook, no door will ever open for me again. I wait for the day to dawn, for a shot to ring out, to get it over with. *Eliminé*.

I have no conclusion to give to this report. *She* says she is looking for the author of her days. In her life, the father is like an erratum that crept into a text and confuses it. A typo that weakens the impact of the words. A calamitous lapse. I am charged with hunting down the error, fingering the guilty party, denouncing the one who committed the crime. The crime of having allowed her to open her eyes onto this world without first removing the scales from them.

She wants to give herself another father. It's her latest big idea, her latest wild goose chase. In her life, all wild goose chases take on a tragic cast. She has the particular seriousness of those who have always suspected that there is an irregularity in their being, an irregularity that renders their actions void, annuls their ambitions, sabotages their progress. She will have to choose between these two specimens of father. Between a bestselling novelist's book, a book that puts on a showy display of erudition and seduction, a book written with facility, a book that enchants the reader, a book padded out with frivolous phrases and ending with a pirouette — she has to choose between that charming book and the other specimen, an austere book that encloses nothing but a little dried blood.

She says she wants to dedicate herself to writing in the same way as I have devoted myself to madness — this is an example of the kind of expression her letter is crammed with, it makes her sound like a renegade Carmelite nun. She says she wants to join the underground. Flee from life. Renounce her sensations. Abdicate her desires. Take her pleasure only in her obsessions. To be nothing but a little dessicated body in the service of writing, fertile writing. She doesn't want anything to distract her from this rigor, but still she keeps an eye on temptations. A man goes by and there she is, ready to abandon the great work in order to collect the small change of love. From time to time, she has to leave the underground, she has to go out savior hunting. By choosing to write, she is already saved, she saved herself. She remains afloat but believes she is sinking. She signals to those who are strolling along the bank, to the figures silhouetted against a background of confusion, to the men who take on the look of the father, imitate the father's voice. Inevitably, they run aground trying to save her. She draws them away from the shore for just that purpose: to show them that they are powerless to save her. In the end, they learn that she has no need of a buoy or a lifeguard, that in her own way she is afloat in this sea she herself undammed. The only thing left for them to do is find the strength to make their way back to the shore and thus provide her with the spectacle of an inglorious retreat rather than that of a meaningless drowning. ¶ I owe her a debt. For having set the standard too high, for having presented the love I lived as the only one worth the trouble of attempting, I have to pay. She demands that I make amends. I imprinted in her head the image of a love that has no dealings with the world, that feeds on its own savagery. She seized that love as a model, and that model pushed her away from life. She accuses me of having allowed her to believe that lovers are united by ties of blood, that only blood can separate them. She grew up expecting love to culminate in tragedy, believing that men who love end their days in an asylum, and women at the end of a rope. She believed. Then she saw lovers making other careers for themselves besides madness, she saw lovers committing a skin-deep suicide only to be reborn to a new love. She sees only escapees and survivors. She accuses me of having let her believe that love is a mass grave, a beautiful mass grave. ¶ Meanwhile, she abuses sentimentality. She lives in the hope that one day a man will come, that he will have the father's face, the father's profile, the father's voice, that he will come in, shut the door behind him, and dedicate himself to her to the point of nausea. As she nourishes this hope, she puts all her energy into defending herself against the coming of the savior. She pushes him out of her way, she alienates the clientele, she wants to eat out of love's hand and give nothing in return. She waylays passersby who try frantically to tempt her with offers of happiness, only the better to send them back to their insignificance. They offer her nothing but a life without history. Meanwhile, she has stored up plans for destruction, prescriptions for death. She'll end up alone and crazy. Meanwhile, she abuses sentimentality, she poisons her head, she lives on a diet of distress alone.

She asks me to give her reasons for no longer wanting to *go away*. Eclipsing herself is her obsession. Because she came in without being seen, she wants to make a spectacle of her exit. She's one of those women who want to die because they feel sorry for themselves. She asks me, a man who was banished, for a license to exist. She asks me, a man who's been adrift for a very long time now, to find a foothold for her. She demands that I inject her with new hopes. She would like to die, but she still believes in happiness. She makes as if to go away, but she hopes a miracle will block her path as she heads for the abyss. I have no crown to give her, no consolation to bring her. I'm nothing but a piece of recycled garbage that still remembers the dump.

Sixth night. A week's reprieve spent in this icy room smoking cigarette after cigarette, rereading the letter's distinguished handwriting, sleeping with my back against the shelves, questioning books without hearing an echo of response. The letter awaits its reply. I am not in possession of the truth. Images surge up, I no longer know if they were brought by the wind or by memory or if they blossomed on the dungheap of madness. The report I'm going to send is unfinished. And who knows, I may hide the gray notebook somewhere in the library, squeezed between two books. There will be no revelation. Truth's mouth is toothless, its breath is foul. The secrets it turns and turns between tongue and palate smell like bad food gone stale.

148

*   *   *

Before I wrap myself up in my coat tomorrow night, I'll
pull all the books down from the shelves and arrange
them around me in a half-circle. I'll light a cigarette and
fall asleep, forgetting to put it out. No one will come and
ask my ashes to account for anything. No one will demand
the truth from my charred remains. My body will be one
with the books.

32

Ricin knocks at the door. I pick up my coat and the package that's on the table and follow him. The package arrived this morning from Corrèze. It's the size of a large notebook, wrapped in brown paper and tied with string. (Write to the uncle, Ricin had said, He will give you the panacea for your urge for a father. Your mother threw a pile of secrets in front of your door. You wanted to dig a hole and hide them all. But as you dug, you found other secrets. To avoid striking against their corpses, you resigned yourself to digging another hole. And here you are now with a new pile. Brave little soldier, digging trenches to make war on herself! You have to write to the uncle, the mad archivist, and you have to agree to live with a pile of secrets near the door. Otherwise you're going to spend your life digging up secrets only to bury them again immediately. You'll dig holes, you'll go from secret to lie, you'll no longer see the light of day and you'll end up like all the rodents in every family saga: you'll be dying, your belly swollen with poison.) On the envelope, my name and the address were written in capital letters with a thick black pencil. No indication of the sender. I clutch the package against me (*We seek treasures with avid hands and we're glad when we find earthworms*). I go down the stairs. Ricin goes ahead of me. No one lurks in front of the building waiting for us to appear any more. I'm going to leave this apartment, this street, this neighborhood. Ricin doesn't know I intend to slip away. It's our last nocturnal walk. He paces beside me, cigarette in his fingers. He has hollow cheeks, his hair falls into a point at the back of his neck. The skin of his throat is wrinkled in several places. He doesn't like the way I'm looking at him. He turns his head aside and takes a long pull on his cigarette. Ricin walks on my left, I sense a presence to my right. On the sidewalk opposite, I can see the silhouette of a large black dog between the cars at the stoplight. Ricin hasn't seen it. The dog walks with its head low. At the corner, Ricin goes left, the dog goes right and walks away. I turn around. By now, the dog is nothing but a black shape at the end of the avenue. I hand Ricin the package I was clutching. *I'm leaving.* I turn back, I follow the dog's trail. He's moving fast along the tree-lined avenue. I quicken my step. I feel the rush of cold wind against my cheeks. *I'm leaving.*

Afterword

As a young girl attending a French lycée in Vietnam,
"I felt rootless in my own country," Linda Lê has said.
"At home they spoke Vietnamese, but I knew nothing
about Vietnamese literature, I had nothing in common
with the other children my age; I have always been a foreigner." Born in Da Lat and raised in Saigon, Linda Lê
has spent half her thirty years in France, where she arrived at the age of fourteen, a refugee. In her work there
are no easy distinctions between foreign and native, between the immigrant and the member of the dominant
culture; all the characters she is interested in, whatever
their national or racial origins, are fundamentally detached from the worlds they inhabit, living in exile, even
in their putative homelands. ¶ The stance of the outsider,
the person who remains at the margins, is, of course, not
new in French literature; one can find Lê's antecedents in
writers as diverse as Céline, Artaud, Camus, Rimbaud,
Nerval. Nor is she the first writer of non-French extrac-
tion to embrace the French language as her only possible
homeland: think of Beckett, Ionesco, Cioran . . . But to
label her work with the name of a school of contempo-
rary French letters, a movement, a style of writing, or a
group of writers, is impossible. There, too, she does not fit
in, and quite deliberately. ¶ One might, for example, try
to align *Slander*, her fifth novel (a sixth, in a completely
different vein, has since been published), with the *autofiction* lately so successful in France — the fictionalized
autobiography practiced by Marguerite Duras, Philippe
Sollers, Serge Dubrovsky, and others. Lê makes no attempt to conceal the autobiographical nature of some of
the material here, but it has been reworked to a far more
radical degree than in *autofiction*, reduced to one voice

among many in the novel's polyglossia. And Lê's attitude toward her own autobiography is another disparity: her radical lucidity, her urgent need to demask, extends even to her own most cherished assumptions. She herself is not safe from her will to puncture every grand illusion; indeed, she is in greater danger than anyone else, constantly doubling back on herself to check for self-delusions, to uncover the petty melodrama that coexists with every weighty emotion. ¶ The inclusion of Lê's work in the category of what has been called *la francophonie asiatique* is equally problematic. That literature, produced by Vietnamese writers who wrote in French, began in the 1920s with Nguyen Van Nho's *Souvenirs d'un étudiant* and reached its apogee in the 1950s and 1960s, most notably in the works of Pham Van Ky; it dealt primarily — for obvious historical and political reasons — with Vietnamese cultural difference in the context of the political environment and events of French colonialism (see Jack Yeager, *The Vietnamese Novel in French: A Literary Response to Colonialism*, University Press of New England, 1987). But rather than existing in the state of suspension between two cultures, belonging fully to neither, that is the locus of Vietnamese Francophone literature, Lê's work defiantly announces its contempt for the idea of "fully belonging" to any culture. When, in *Slander*, the uncle, the "madman without a country," says "We are from Nowhere, *she* and I," it isn't a plaintive statement of defeat and rejection, but an almost triumphant affirmation of escape, freedom. ¶ If Vietnamese Francophone writers such as Pham Van Ky, Pham Duy Khiem, and Nguyen Tien Lang are in any sense the forerunners of Lê's writing, they are not an influence she avows. Her most passionately expressed enthusiasm is for the literature and art of Austria, in particular the work of Thomas Bernhard and Ingeborg Bachmann. Other preferred readings include Kafka, Nietszche, and Schopenhauer, E. M. Cioran, the Rumanian philosopher who wrote in French, and the *Intimate Diary* of the Swiss writer Henri Frédéric Amiel. A number of recent French translations have enabled Lê at last to become acquainted with Vietnamese literature, and to admire, in particular, the work of Pham Thi Hoai and Nguyen Huy Thiep. There has been a reciprocal interest in her work in Vietnam, but a translation of *Slander* into Vietnamese was deemed too controversial, and the project was cancelled.

Someone else might understandably boast about having produced six novels by the age of 30. Lê seems embarrassed by it; in conversation, she dismisses her three earliest works (as if having produced a mere three novels by 30 were something almost everyone does). Her latest novel, *Les dits d'un idiot* [The sayings of an idiot, 1995], contains a lengthy denunciation of a writer for having written too many books "for nothing," books that are "too green," that are "half spoiled," that were published only to lengthen the list of "Other Works by the Same Author" that will appear in the next book. Few writers would so publicly and so undeservingly take themselves to task for their own fertility. ¶ Another characteristic of Lê's writing is the skein of allusions, literary, philosophical, and artistic, that interpenetrates the text. Far from being the manifestations of a self-congratulatory erudition, however, these allusions often serve to underscore Lê's own unease in the role of author. As a passage in her fourth novel, *Les évangiles du crime* [The gospels of crime, 1992], puts it: "To write a book: nothing is easier when one has a bloodhound's nose (the hunt for the finest morsels of prose demands an alert mind), a pickpocket's dexterity (I steal very deftly, in such a way that even the owner, the book's author, is grateful for my discretion), a makeup artist's skill (the laboratory where I write is a recycling center for all the texts that have been forgotten), and a

small-time gangster's cynicism (the plagiarist extols himself for his petty larcenies in the name of the great crimes
he abstains from committing — and what greater crime
than still to believe in literature in this century?)" ¶ The
trajectory of her writing thus far has been a relentless ex-
perimentation with new structures and styles, an absolute
refusal to establish a single, characteristic narrative tech-
nique and continue working it. In this, too, Lê insists on
challenging herself anew at every step. "Each book corre-
sponds to a phase of my inner evolution," Lê says, "and
every time it's a victory, both over the preceding book and
over what I had lived until then. Otherwise, it wouldn't be
worth the trouble of writing."

Slander is the first of Linda Lê's books to appear in
English. I would like to express my gratitude to Michael
Moore, Adrienne Coppola, Carlota Lozada, and Kim and
Theo Landsman for their advice, understanding, and as-
sistance during the translation process. I would also like
to thank Monique Chefdor, without whom I might never
have learned French or begun translating. Above all, I
thank Linda Lê for her extraordinarily kind and helpful
comments, explanations, and suggestions, and for having
set the standard this translation struggles to meet.

In the European Women Writers series

The Delta Function
By Rosa Montero
Translated and with an afterword
by Kari Easton and
Yolanda Molina Gavilán

Music from a Blue Well
By Torborg Nedreaas
Translated by Bibbi Lee

Nothing Grows by Moonlight
By Torborg Nedreaas
Translated by Bibbi Lee

Candy Story
By Marie Redonnet
Translated by Alexandra Quinn

Forever Valley
By Marie Redonnet
Translated by Jordan Stump

Hôtel Splendid
By Marie Redonnet
Translated by Jordan Stump

Nevermore
By Marie Redonnet
Translated by Jordan Stump

Rose Mellie Rose
By Marie Redonnet
Translated by Jordan Stump

Why Is There Salt in the Sea?
By Brigitte Schwaiger
Translated by Sieglinde Lug

The Same Sea As Every Summer
By Esther Tusquets
Translated by Margaret E. W.
Jones

DATE DUE
